Saved by a Barbarian

NOT-SO-SAVAGE BARBARIANS
BOOK TWO

AMY PADILLA

Copyright © 2025 by Amy Padilla

All rights reserved. No part of this book may be reproduced or used in any manner without written permission of the copyright owner except for the use of quotations in a book review. For more information:

authoramypadilla@gmail.com

authoramypadilla.com

PA & Social Media Manager: Aspen Tree E.A.S.

TRIGGER WARNING

The following series contains potentially upsetting themes, such as dubious consent, threats of & violence against the MC, and attempted assault.

Extra warning: This book contains a scene of ignoring withdrawal of consent. If this is at all upsetting to you, please consider skipping Chapter One.

Consent is sexy and your mental health is very important! If these themes are at all triggering to you, please consider another book.

One

"Come on, Patrick. You have to forgive me. I know I acted like an ass, but I was just a kid. I was scared."

He said that, but Richard Oberon the third was the bane of my existence when we were kids. He tormented me. He and his friends. They spent years making sure I was miserable. I wanted to believe him. I didn't want to be bitter for the rest of my life. It was just hard. He was a bully.

"How do I know this isn't a trick?" I asked cautiously.

"Why would I ever say it out loud if it wasn't real? I don't want to end up hanged." He stepped closer, taking my hands in his and rubbing his thumbs over my knuckles. My heart twinged. I had hidden away that part of me for years. I wasn't sure how to handle the kind of attention he was giving me. And it was hard to focus on staying strong when he was so sweet to me.

"This is real. I've wanted you for years. You're the only one for me. And now that we're adults, we can make it work. Give me a chance."

Swallowing hard around the lump in my throat, I searched his face. We were nearly the same height. I'd been smaller when we were younger, which always made him seem huge and intimidating. Now that I'd gone through my last growth spurt, we could look each other in the eye. It put us on more equal ground, and it made me connect with him in ways I didn't expect.

I saw the fear, the heartache. He put himself at risk by exposing his nature to me. If I didn't share that nature, it would've been dangerous for him. Being like us wasn't legal in our town. There were very few towns that allowed it. I'd been planning to save up enough to move to a safer one, to finally live my life, but it'd take time. Spending that whole period alone and hiding wasn't a pleasant thought. And if Richard was like me, maybe he'd want to come with me.

"I... I forgive you."

His relief was instantaneous, his shoulders slumped as the weight of his guilt sloughed off. And his smile... Richard had always been handsome, even as a little kid. But whenever he smiled, it gave me butterflies. Combined with the relief he felt, his smile was almost blinding.

Yanking me closer, he hugged me tight, and I wrapped my arms around him to comfort him. He wasn't shaking or anything, he was too brave for that, but I felt the tension in his body. He was obviously upset.

When he pulled away, he looked excited. "So, we're together then, right? We can, uh... try some stuff? I've always been too scared to ask, but I feel like I can trust you. You know what it's like to want something you can't have."

My cheeks burned at his comment. "Y-yes, I understand. Um... I'm not sure—"

He pouted at me, those big blue eyes widening in a pleading expression that did funny things to my heart. "Come on... I'm twenty-three and have never been touched. It's a travesty, Patrick. My hand can only help so much."

In the back of my head, a little voice said it was too fast to do anything with Richard. He only just apologized and confessed to me. But we were the same age, and it was awful not being able to get close to someone without fearing them turning you in to the warden. And thinking about Richard touching himself was a little hot, honestly. Who could think about that and not get turned on?

"Richard..." I protested, albeit quietly and without much strength behind it. He stepped closer. I felt his erection press against my hip, and my whole body quivered with long-repressed want. Would one night be so bad? We could talk more after, and figure out how we wanted this to work. He couldn't just come out and say we were friends after years of bullying me without people getting suspicious. It would take a while for us to establish ourselves as good enough friends to see each other regularly. Who knew when we'd next get the opportunity? Did I want to give up the chance to finally experience intimacy just because things were so new with us?

Grinding himself against me, he leaned to whisper in my ear. "Come on, baby. We'll start off simple. Get on our knees for each other. Don't you want to explore with me?"

My knees went a little weak at his suggestion. Yes. I did want that. I heard about things men and women did together, and I always imagined what it'd be like to do it with a man. It was like my sexually repressed side took over my mind and made me a little reckless because I found myself nodding and melting when Richard smiled at me again.

This was a good thing. Things were going to change for me. My business was doing well, which made my father resent me less, and I finally had someone who wanted to be with me. It was worth the risk.

"You go first," he cajoled, nudging me a little further back against the hedge. When he'd asked me to meet him out here during a party, I thought he'd start bullying me again. I was determined to stand up to him for once. I never thought we'd end up like this.

"Shouldn't we… I don't know… kiss first?"

I dreamed most often about kissing. About what it would be like to feel someone's lips against mine, their arms wrapped around me. The image always warmed me to my core, and I desperately wanted to feel it for real. But Richard was nervous and impatient, glancing over his shoulder towards the house a few times.

"I'm not sure how long we have until someone comes looking, Patrick. Let's just do it, alright? I'll make it up to you later."

He was right, of course. Richard was a popular man. He had lots of friends. There was no telling how long it would be before someone came looking for him. There wasn't enough time to explore everything, and from the way he ground against me, he obviously needed relief. I did too, if I was being honest. I could wait for a kiss. Hopefully, we could meet up often and explore somewhere more private so we could take our time with that part.

My heart pounded in my chest and my stomach clenched with nerves as I sank to my knees. Richard's eyes lit up, and he raced to free his erection from his trousers. His giddy excitement filled my belly with butterflies. He really was quite handsome. And after tonight, he would be mine, even if no one else knew. It would be a secret we shared between us.

My breath caught in my throat when he finally freed himself. I'd seen a cock before, obviously, since I had one myself, but never another person's. It was a heady feeling, and my hand shook when I reached to touch him for the first time. He wasn't overly large, which was kind of shocking, actually. With the way he strutted around, I kind of figured he'd be bigger. I resisted the urge to compare him to myself. It didn't matter. His foreskin was retracted, he was obviously desperate, and if I didn't get on with it, there wouldn't be enough time for him to touch me too.

I was tentative at first, licking along the head and down his length. I wasn't entirely sure what I was doing. I had never seen the act myself to be able to mimic it.

"Suck on it," Richard demanded, his voice gruff. When I looked up at him, he looked impatient, and the shadows played with his expression enough to remind me of the cruel looks he gave me when he was mocking me. It made me hesitate, but then his face softened, and he ran his fingers gently through my hair, cupping the back of my head. "Come on. I want a turn with you, too."

Excited by the prospect, I bent my head to the task, sucking his cock into my mouth. The taste was salty but not entirely unpleasant. He was a little musty, though, which wasn't enticing. I chalked it up to nerves about telling me about his nature that made him sweat so much. Ignoring the smell, I sucked a little more into my mouth, shivering when Richard groaned quietly.

"That's it. Take more. Keep going."

My whole body flushed with excitement, and I felt my prick leaking in my smallclothes. If I wasn't careful, Richard wouldn't get a chance to have a turn before I reached completion. It was just so exciting finally touching a man like this. And the way he spoke—

Suddenly, the hand that had been gently cupping the back of my head fisted my hair instead, gripping to the point of pain. Tears stung my eyes at the painful touch, but before I could release Richard's cock to complain, he shoved me against him, forcing the entirety of his cock into my mouth. The smell was overwhelming with my nose pressed to his groin and he forced himself so abruptly deep, it hurt. The combination triggered my gag reflex, and I tried to pull away, but Richard wouldn't allow it. He thrust his hips, groaning and telling me how good it felt. I'd enjoy the commentary more if it didn't hurt so much. I finally yanked myself free, gasping for air, and I flinched when I looked up at Richard and he reached completion all over my face.

"R-Richard!" I protested, my throat hoarse. I still had to get home, and it wasn't safe for either of us if I looked debauched.

His chuckle was familiar and cruel, and when I mopped my face with my handkerchief and looked up at him again, he looked triumphant.

"Richard?"

Tucking himself away, he gave me a vicious smile. "I always knew. I think most of the town knew. But the mayor is a stickler, and we never had any proof. We do now."

"W-what are you talking about?"

His head tipped, and his smile widened as his friends came around the hedge, leering at me.

"You see, I have all these witnesses now. I'll be able to tell the mayor that you got me drunk and took advantage. Forced yourself on me. Then we'll finally be able to rid this town of your filth. You'll be hanged for this, you know. You should come to terms with it now, Patrick. You brought this on yourself."

Horror and terror warred in my gut, freezing me where I knelt. On the ground at their feet, like I had been my entire life. I was a fool to have trusted him. So starved for love and affection that I willfully believed the man who tormented me my whole life wanted me. I should have questioned things more when he refused to kiss me.

"Here." One of Richard's friends offered him a glass of wine. "Spill this on your shirt. It will make things more realistic. And don't forget to slur and stumble." He tousled Richard's hair to make him look mussed and ripped open his shirt for good measure. They had it all planned out. They were so desperate to get rid of me. Why? What did I ever do to them?

My gaze flicked back toward the house. I couldn't run in there. No one would believe me. I wasn't even sure I got all the seed off my face. But I couldn't stay here either. Not without facing the noose. My gaze shifted again, this time over my shoulder. We were on the edge of the mayor's property. A few dozen meters away stood the forest. I had no other choice. It was the only possible chance I had to survive.

So while they were distracted getting Richard ready for his big acting debut, I ran. And I didn't look back.

Two

"It's my turn," I murmured low, nudging Rath with a mock scowl.

His smug smirk was irritating, but being my best friend and the best hunter in the entire clan, he'd technically earned it. I'd lost track of the number of times I'd missed a shot and he'd taken down the beast I'd been aiming for. Not this time, though. I was going to get the biggest kill, and he would finally acknowledge my prowess. Or at least stop teasing me so often.

Drawing back the string of my bow, I aimed for the sorvik that stood grazing a short distance away. I had the shot lined up perfectly, and excitement filled my gut at the possibility of taking it down. But when I released my arrow, the beast chose that exact moment to move to another patch of grass. Causing me to miss entirely.

The animal startled and took off, and I wasn't fast enough to pull out another arrow before a much larger one shot through the trees and hit the sorvik dead on. I dropped my head forward in defeat. Of course, Rath took it down so effortlessly. Everything was easy for him.

He patted my shoulder affectionately. "Be at ease, Verus. Your luck will improve."

I made a face, pushing to my feet so I could follow him toward where the animal had fallen. He was such a noble opponent. It made it hard to be cross with him.

"I think I dislike you a little more each day. It was my kill."

He grunted, picking up the animal and tossing it over my shoulder. "Then you can take it back to the village. I will find another before returning."

I shook my head, offering it back to him. "No. You have a bondmate waiting for you. You got your kill. Go back to him and let me hunt more. I'll at least find some zorvash before I head back."

He nodded, taking any excuse he could to get back to his bondmate. They had their bonding ceremony several months ago, just before the first snows fell, but they were still smitten and wrapped around each other at every free moment. It made me smile to see it, knowing how lonely Rath had been before he met Finn. They belonged together, and I was happy for my brother for finding his bondmate. Their love made me consider looking for a bondmate myself soon. Maybe the next batch of tributes would bring another male.

After sending Rath off with his prize, I headed deeper into the forest. It was vast, and someone could easily get lost inside it if they weren't careful, but I knew it like the back of my hand. Every winter, our clan settled against the forest for better hunting during the colder months. We would be moving on soon enough, now that spring was finally upon us, and I loved our way of life on the move, but I would miss the forest until we returned. It was always so calm inside.

As if to prove the notion false, I heard a terrified scream ring through the air. My instincts had my feet moving before I even made the full decision to do so. I raced toward the sound, leaping over fallen trees and roots. I quickly saw what had made such a horrific noise. Someone was running through the trees. Not a clan brother, nor anyone I recognized, but I couldn't get a decent look at them before they tripped over something and fell down a small ditch, their body disappearing behind a bush. I hurried forward, and my breath caught in my throat when I saw what they were running from.

Shadowstalker.

They didn't come near our hunting grounds often, but they were tenacious. It was what made them dangerous. They were not the largest, nor the most threatening, with only small claws and larger teeth to assist them in a hunt. It was their refusal to give up that gave them their name. Once they decided to hunt something, they would not stop until death; theirs or their prey's. Brothers had been dragged off in their sleep because of these creatures. And there was only one way to deal with them.

Unsheathing my sword, I pushed my muscles harder to reach the shadowstalker in time. They were fast, but not impossible to catch. It leapt into the air, and the person it was stalking screamed again, but I caught it in time, tackling the animal to the ground with a shout.

Being so much smaller than me, the creature managed to wriggle free, putting more space between us. Its gaze flicked constantly over my shoulder to its prey, splitting its focus. I bared my teeth at it, keeping my stance low. It would not be deterred so easily, but it was more cautious now, knowing I stood between it and its next meal.

It hissed at me in warning, posturing to get me to back down. So I hissed back. It seemed to anger the creature, and it lunged at me. I did the same, blocking its claws with my arm as I sliced through its middle. I would need a visit to the healers for that, but it was worth the injury when the animal shuddered out its last breath and went limp.

When I was sure it wasn't faking to get me to lower my guard, I pushed to my feet again. It wasn't a sorvik, but shadowstalker meat was hearty in a stew. It would feed some of my clan at the very least.

A whimper drew my attention over my shoulder. I turned just in time to watch the unfamiliar man's eyes roll back in his head as he collapsed.

"Kaiza," I cursed low, rushing to his side. I checked for any signs the shadowstalker had already got to him, but all his injuries were meager in comparison to the creature's normal attacks. Small cuts, as though he'd rolled through a thorn bush or two, some bruising, and a tear in his trousers along the knee, likely due to his recent fall. His clothes were soiled and, from his unkempt appearance, I guessed he'd been out here a few days at least. Alone? Why? He was not a hunter. He was not dressed for the weather that still dipped at night. He had no weapons on him. From the looks of him, I didn't think he was prepared for entering the forest at all.

Underneath the dirt and mud, the clothing he wore looked fancy, like what they wore in the nearby towns.

I reached out to brush a lock of his hair away from his face, flinching when I felt how cold his skin was. I had a great many questions, but he needed care first. Besides, if he truly was from a nearby town, he would not speak our tongue. I would need someone to translate for me.

Carefully, so as not to disturb any unseen injuries, I lifted him into my arms. He was not a slight man, more curvy and thick. Not heavy, not for me anyway, but not as thin as Finn. The meat on him was probably the reason he lasted so long out here alone. He didn't stir, and his head lolled when I stood, but I could feel his shallow breath upon my skin. He was alright for the time being.

With him in my arms, it was a pain to also grab the shadowstalker, but I refused to leave the kill behind. Unlike the man, who was larger but light enough in my arms, the shadowstalker was small and dense, and my forearm burned, carrying it by the scruff one handed. I was grateful when we reached the gathering tree where my stallion waited.

"Dhellgas, my dear friend. We have another passenger this day. We need to make haste to return to the clan."

The stallion bobbed his head like he understood me. Godr, the horse-master of our clan, believed they did. As he was my best friend's brother, I listened to his counsel and always treated Dhellgas as though he understood me. He was sometimes feisty and petulant if I didn't often bring him farther into the forest to join the hunt, but he was a good stallion and an excellent listener when I was drunk and needed someone to complain to.

Unlike townsfolk, who used leather seats on their animals, we rode without. It was why we brought our kills to the gathering tree, as it was close enough to the village that we didn't need to worry about hurting our stallions with the extra weight. I had to set down the man while I draped the shadowstalker on Dhellgas's back, ignoring the flick of his tail to show his annoyance. Shadowstalkers were heavy.

"I will tell Godr to give you an extra treat for carrying us. Be at ease, my brother."

This settled him, and he stood patiently while I gathered the man up again and jumped onto his back. Once the male was safely tucked against me, I patted Dhellgas's hide to urge him forward.

"Make haste. He needs a healer."

As we rode, I looked down at the male in my arms. His skin was pale, and he had dark circles under his eyes, but if you looked past that, he was a sweet-looking man. He had hair the color of the setting sun and spots on his cheeks and nose. His lips were petal pink and soft looking, and his eyelashes were long, resting delicately on his rounded cheeks. My chest tightened a little, looking down at him. What were the chances that I was considering searching for a bondmate and happened to stumble upon him in the forest alone and in need of protection? It seemed almost too good to be true.

Three

Voices around me brought me out of unconsciousness. Exhaustion pulled at my senses, urging me to go back to sleep, but the last thing I remembered was the growl of that terrifying creature in the forest as it chased me. There were no people. So then where…?

I forced my eyes open, despite how heavy they felt. The room I was in was bright, lit by an open fire in the middle with a hole above it to let the smoke out. It was warm too, and after days of being cold, it felt so good, I whimpered. The sound drew the attention of the people standing nearby; a woman with long skirts and a rounded belly, and two enormous men with hair shaved on the sides and symbols inked on their skin. Barbarians.

Fear and horror flooded my system, and I sat up abruptly. It all came back to me in a rush. The creature that had been stalking me had lunged at me, and a barbarian man with huge muscles and a slightly curved sword jumped in between us, knocking the creature away. After watching the barbarian growl and hiss at the creature like an animal, I wasn't sure which to be more frightened of. And when he sliced the creature almost in half, it was too much for me to handle after what felt like countless days in constant terror. My consciousness slipped away from me just as he stood, towering so far above me it looked as though he was as tall as the trees.

He must have brought me back with him. I'd heard the stories of the barbarians. They were dangerous, violent, and only a treaty between the towns and their clans kept us all safe. A treaty I may have broken by accidentally stumbling onto their land. Panic swelled in my chest, and I looked around for a way out. Maybe if I ran far away, they'd—

"Shh… It's okay," the woman said, her hands up like she was trying to soothe a wild horse. I shrank away from her, my eyes constantly flicking over her shoulder to the men that stood behind her. One was familiar, the one I'd seen in the forest. The other looked older but no less intimidating. They both watched me with deep frowns. I probably offended them by ending up here. Maybe it would've been better to let the warden take me instead. At least a hanging would be quick.

I shifted to get to my feet, the panic making me want to run, but moving my right leg hurt, and I flinched automatically, crying out in pain.

The barbarian appeared at my side in an instant. I never even saw him move. He said something I didn't understand, nudging me back onto the pallet of blankets they had me on. The woman sighed, exasperated.

"I'm sorry. They've got intense protective instincts, and you're hurt. Please don't be scared. You're not in any danger here."

"W-where am I?"

The older barbarian stepped forward, his words heavily accented but easily understood. "Our clan currently rests against the edge of the forest. We are a great distance from any town. Where did you come from?"

I opened my mouth to answer automatically before thinking better of it. I didn't want them to send me back there. If the woman was right and they weren't going to hurt me, I wanted to be sent somewhere that I had a chance at living a normal life. Starting over with no money would be hard, but at least I would live through the week.

"I… I'm sorry for coming into your territory. I didn't mean to. I'll leave—"

The barbarian next to me spoke again, his brows furrowed in confusion. He didn't understand me. Which was strange, since the few times I'd seen the barbarians come to retrieve their tribute, they always spoke our language.

The woman shook her head at him, but he didn't like that answer. He said something else, more demanding this time, and her expression flattened in annoyance. She answered back in his language, her voice terse, and when he bared his teeth at her, I shrank back automatically. He noticed the movement and whipped his head around, a pained expression flashing over his face when I flinched. Before I had a chance to blink, I felt his hands underneath me, pulling me off the bed of blankets and into his arms. Pain and panic shot through me, and I shot a terrified look at the woman who'd been speaking to me, my voice warbling as tears filled my eyes.

"Please. I didn't mean to. Don't let them hurt me."

She launched to her feet, yelling at the barbarian who held me cradled against his chest. I didn't understand anything that they were saying, and the older barbarian didn't speak my language either when he joined the conversation. All I could focus on was the fact that the barbarian's arms didn't even tremble, holding my weight the entire time they argued with each other. Like I wasn't at all heavy to him.

I knew that wasn't true. It was one of Richard's favorite things to torment me about. I'd always been chubby. Even as a kid, I weighed the most. Combined with my short stature, it made me the center of plenty of ridicule. Even when I had a growth spurt and my weight balanced a little, I was still thick. And yet the barbarian didn't even have to readjust me. Was my weight negligible to him?

The barbarian's voice grew louder, more determined, and his grip on me tightened as he took a step back. Frightened, I looked at the other two. The woman shot me an apologetic look.

"I'm sorry. He's not going to hurt you. He says you need a protector and won't let anyone else take the job. I told him you aren't a tribute, and it doesn't work that way for visitors, but he's refusing to see reason."

I didn't know much about tributes, but there weren't any male ones, that I knew about anyway. Besides, I hadn't volunteered for it, even if there were. I wasn't supposed to be here. The terrifying creature in the forest had herded me in this direction, and I accidentally ended up here. But now a barbarian was determined to keep me here, despite my protests and the protests of the woman who was trying to help me. And before anyone could get him to listen to reason, he ducked out of the tent and stormed off with me in his arms.

I was trembling when he brought me into another tent. This one was smaller. It looked like it was only meant for one person. It had a messy pallet of blankets, a small wooden chest, and a table with a lantern on it, but that was it. When he set me on the bed, my panic compounded, and I tried to lunge away, tears streaming down my cheeks.

"No, no! Please!"

The townsfolk said plenty about how the barbarians forced themselves on the tributes. If he saw me as one too, he'd treat me the same way.

All of this because I was too stupid to realize Richard was playing me for a fool. I should have ignored his request and gone home. Was I truly so desperate for affection that I lost my mind the minute someone treated me with any form of kindness?

It hurt, trying to get away from him. My leg burned with white-hot pain. But I couldn't just sit there and take it. I slapped at his hands as he tried to grab me, tears streaming down my face. He was saying something, and it almost sounded like he was trying to soothe me, but I couldn't understand the words. For all I knew, he was telling me just to not move and take it.

For a split second, he got the upper hand, knocking me back and pinning my wrists against the bedding. He spoke again, shaking his head, but he couldn't get more than a few words out before his weight disappeared, and he was gone. I sat up with a cry, scrambling to get to my feet so I could run for the exit, but my right knee buckled when I tried to put weight on it, and I collapsed near the flap of the tent.

The flap ripped open and the woman from before hurried in, helping me to turn over. I clutched at my knee, gritting my teeth against the pain. It was so intense, it made me feel nauseous. When the woman tried to touch it, I pushed her hands away, choking on sobs.

"P-please! Just let me go! I'm sorry! Just let me go!"

"I'm afraid I can't do that. You're too hurt to go anywhere right now. I'm sorry. You'll have to stay here for now."

Here? Where a barbarian carried me off to his tent to do god knows what to me while ignoring everyone else? Where I could still hear him shouting and arguing with whoever was outside the tent? I'd rather deal with the pain and take my chances in the forest.

Suddenly, I heard a yelp and the sound of a scuffle before the world outside the tent went quiet. I held my breath, terrified, and for a few moments, it was quiet before footsteps approached the tent again. But the man who poked his head in wasn't who I was expecting. He was too small to be a barbarian. He barely looked old enough to be considered an adult. He had wide blue eyes and curly hair that was shaved on the sides, and when he stepped fully into the tent, I could tell he was shorter than me. Shorter, more slender, and a little shy, biting his lip as he bounced on his toes.

"Wh-who are you?"

He offered me a small smile. "I'm Finn. The first male tribute."

Four

"B-but tributes are only female."

I didn't understand. I'd never heard of a male tribute before.

He nodded and shrugged. "They were. Until me. I came to the clan during the last tribute gathering. Orthorr thought talking to me might help you since Verus won't let the whole protector thing go. My bondmate took him to cool off, so we've got a minute. Are you okay?"

I was… confused. And scared. None of them acted concerned that the barbarian who took me wouldn't let the idea of a protector go. I didn't know what it meant, and after the way he pinned me, I was afraid it was something they'd just come to accept. I didn't want to accept it. I'd gone my whole life without being touched like that. I didn't want my first experience to be forced and traumatizing. I'd been traumatized enough after what happened with Richard. I just wanted to escape and find my way to a town that would accept me.

"He's injured," the woman answered for me. "I didn't want to undress him before he was awake to consent, but his leg is obviously hurt, and what little I could see of the bruising in the rip of his trousers, I'm worried it might be broken. I'll need to set it and wrap it up, and check for any other injuries. I *planned* to do it in the healing tent, but then Verus lost his ever-loving mind."

Finn made a face. "Yeah, I've never seen him like that before." He turned to me and smiled softly again. "He's taken a liking to you."

"I-I don't want him to like me! I don't want to be here! I need to leave before he comes back! Please!"

Finn grimaced, shaking his head. "Sorry. I didn't mean it like that. He's not going to hurt you. I know the rumors about the barbarians say otherwise, but they don't rape people here. At least not in this clan. I haven't actually met any others. But here, it's considered a heinous crime, and it's punishable by death."

"Then why—" I gestured sharply to the bed where the barbarian pinned me down.

"He brought you here to his tent because that's what they normally do when a new tribute arrives," Finn explained with a sigh. "Tributes get assigned a protector, who keeps them away from the clan for about a week so they can acclimate without getting overwhelmed. Their protectors teach them the language and things about the clan and keep them safe."

That sounded weird, because what if the barbarian was dangerous? They could be hurting the women for a week straight without anyone knowing.

"He doesn't believe me," Finn said quietly to the woman. He bit his lip, his brows furrowed tightly. "I can show him what I've been working on, but I'm not sure it'll help. He's in a weird circumstance. How often does the clan get visitors who aren't other barbarians?"

The woman shook her head. "Never? I've never seen one, at least. Just your brother showing up to get you was a shock to the clan. No one had ever been brave enough to do that before."

"Y-your family came to get you? And you stayed?" I asked, incredulous.

Finn wrinkled his nose. "My brother doesn't actually care about me. He saw me being sent here as a stain on our family's reputation. He didn't want our family name tainted by the idea of me living in sin with a man, even if I was volunteered as a tribute. I stayed because I love it here. I can be myself, be in love with a man without facing a death sentence, and truly live. Nothing was waiting for me back home except pain and ridicule. I didn't want to go back."

It felt like a gut punch when he admitted that out loud. "It's... It's legal here?"

The woman nodded, her face full of warmth. "All kinds of relationships are allowed here. Bonding is sacred and not something a clan leader would ever try to dictate as wrong or right. Finn might be the first male tribute, but he's not the first male attracted to other males."

My mind swam with all the new information, making me a little dizzy. That, combined with the pain still throbbing in my leg, and I couldn't take it anymore. I burst into tears, hugging my arms around myself to try and hold it all in. I was hurt, confused, scared, and it was just too overwhelming to handle.

IT TOOK MY BROTHERS PHYSICALLY REMOVING ME FROM THE TENT TO GET me away from the frightened male. I wanted to help him almost desperately, but I somehow only seemed to make it worse. It tore me apart inside, and while I understood why my brothers pulled me away, I was still focused only on returning to make it right.

Which was when Rath showed up, threw me over his shoulder like one of his catches, and took me to the river to cool off. And he was not kind about it. He threw me into the water that was cold without the sun's rays upon it, making me gasp as I came up for air.

He crossed his arms over his chest, raising an eyebrow at me. "Have you calmed down, or do I need to dunk you a few times?"

I took a step back automatically. We played that game often as children, and he was always the victor. Getting the upper hand against my best friend was nearly impossible. He was better than me at all things. Including caring for a frightened male.

"What would you have me do?" I demanded, throwing my hand toward the direction of my tent. "He is injured and frightened, and I could tell he wished to run away. He would hurt himself if he did so. I only wanted to get him somewhere he could feel safe."

Rath's fierce expression softened a little. "You wish to protect him. This is an honorable thing. But he is not a frightened tribute resigned to their fate. There is more to his story. You are only scaring him more by taking him away from the healers with no explanation. You need to have more patience."

I couldn't admit to him that I wished the male was a tribute. I wished to have the chance to woo him into choosing me. I was so desperate for it, I stole him away. Something about him called to me, and I wasn't sure I'd get the chance to warm him to me unless I did something about it.

Rath let me leave the river only when I was calm enough to listen. Then he accompanied me back to my tent, holding me back when I heard the heavy sobs coming from inside and tried to rush forward to check on him. I shot a worried look at Rath, but he shook his head at me.

"You have not had a tribute before. My advice is to move slowly. He does not understand you. You have to show him he is safe with you. If you rush, you'll frighten him more."

Oh. I hadn't considered that. I only wanted to reach him faster so I could end his suffering sooner. But Rath would know better than I would. Slowing my pace, I crept into the tent, taking in the three inside. My heart felt as though it was ripping to shreds watching the poor man sob so intensely. I wanted to scoop him up and hold him close, so he felt safe. But it wasn't time for that yet, and I was still soaked. I had to hold myself back.

"Why are you all wet?" Zoya demanded from where she sat beside the male, rubbing his back soothingly. I wanted to do that for him. It hurt that I wasn't allowed.

"He needed to cool off," Rath drawled with a shrug.

Finn's snicker surprised the male, and he finally looked up. When he saw me, true fear flashed across his face, making me wince at the sharp stab of guilt that shot through me like a flaming arrow. He said something, his voice tremulous, and Finn shook his head with a soft smile.

"What does he say?" I asked quietly to Zoya.

"He wants to know if you will hurt him," she replied, frowning at me. "You frightened him before. What were you thinking?"

A pained noise escaped me, and I dropped my head forward to show my regret. "I only wanted to get him to stop so he wouldn't hurt himself," I murmured.

Finn spoke again in his own tongue, perhaps translating for me, but I didn't look up. In my desperation to take care of the male, I made him fear me instead. I gestured to Rath without looking up. He was better with tributes. He was better at everything. He would fix this where I could not.

"Rath will bring him back to the healing tent. I will go so he will not be frightened anymore."

And despite how much it hurt, I turned to leave without looking back.

Perhaps I deserved to be alone.

Five

The barbarian looked... heartbroken. Like he was so remorseful about scaring me, it hurt him physically. Finn told me what he said, about how he only wanted to stop me so I wouldn't hurt myself, and he obviously felt bad about it. I wasn't sure what to do about that, but he did pull me out of the forest. Even after saving me from that creature, he could've just left me there. He was a little forceful about bringing me to his tent, but maybe he was just trying to help?

"W-wait..."

The other barbarian, who somehow managed to be bigger than the two I'd already met, stopped him with a hand on his shoulder. But my barbarian didn't turn around. His shoulders bunched up like he was waiting for me to berate him. I wasn't. I just didn't know what to say.

"What's wrong?" Finn asked, putting his hand on my shoulder supportively. They were being really nice, but I was starting to not feel well because of the pain. Sweat gathered at my temples and every ounce of pressure on my body, down to my clothes, felt like a heavy weight. Finn's hand was gentle, but with how much I hurt, it felt like a boulder, and I felt myself sway because of it.

"Uh oh. Finn, catch his head!"

The world went dark again before I could figure out what was going to happen next.

∼

THE NEXT TIME I WOKE UP, I WAS BACK IN THE FIRST TENT, WITH THE FIRE and the warmth. The pain was subdued, and my leg was set up in a splint to keep me from moving it. I wasn't wearing my clothes anymore, they probably had to remove them to deal with the injury, but the tunic I was wearing was longer and covered me, and there was a blanket over everything but my injured leg, which had a paste on it that looked and smelled like a poultice.

At first, I thought I was alone, but the barbarian who rescued me was sitting near the flap, his entire posture defeated. His head hung low, and his arms rested on his knees, hands loose. At first, I thought he was sleeping, but he sighed heavily at one point, and when I twisted enough, I saw his eyes were open.

He didn't look at me, or even move a muscle, and it gave me a moment to truly look at him. His hair wasn't as long as the other barbarians I'd seen. It was shaved on the sides, and he'd worn it in a small ponytail when I saw him earlier. Now it was down and disheveled, like he'd been running his fingers through it. He wore a thicker tunic, probably because it was still chilly, with sturdy-looking trousers and boots with fur sticking out of them. The tunic was sleeveless, which seemed strange with the thickness to keep him warm. But it showed off his arms and the ink carved into his skin. Blocky swirls of black in designs I couldn't quite decipher with the way I was positioned. I couldn't move much at all, thanks to my leg being splinted like it was.

He must've heard me shifting to get more comfortable because his head whipped up, and it looked like he was about to get up, but then he froze and eased back again. Trying not to scare me?

It was an improvement from before, but it felt awkward having him just stare at me. And I was really thirsty. I looked around for anyone else who might be able to understand me, but there was no one but him.

"I, uh… I'm thirsty…" I murmured, looking anywhere but at him. He didn't immediately move, and when I glanced in his direction, his brows were furrowed in confusion. Shoot. How do you communicate when your languages are completely different?

I clumsily mimicked taking a drink, and his eyes lit up in what I thought was understanding. Slowly, he pushed to his feet, heading around the fire to a table covered in what looked like dried herbs. There was also a pitcher and a cup, and he filled it before carefully bringing it to me. It was almost funny how he tried to keep his distance while handing me the cup. He ended up having to get close anyway, because my hands shook when I tried to bring it to my lips, and I spilled a little before he steadied me with his hands cupping mine.

The water was cool and refreshing, and I drank it all down without taking a breath. In the days in the forest, I wasn't sure what was safe to eat or drink. I managed to scoop handfuls of water from a stream here and there, but I was also afraid to stop moving, worried Richard and his friends were following me, hoping to drag me back for a public execution. My town loved those. I found a few berry bushes too, but most plants were unfamiliar to me so far into the forest. I didn't know if they were safe to eat. So I was starving as well as thirsty.

My stomach rumbled so loudly it sounded like that creature in the forest. The barbarian's gaze drifted down and his brow furrowed before he asked a question I didn't understand. When I shook my head to show my confusion, he mimicked eating with his hand and his mouth. I nodded yes. Communicating with him gave me a new appreciation for the spoken word. It was difficult to get points across using only gestures.

He got up as slow as molasses again, creeping towards the exit like he was afraid to make any sudden moves. I found myself biting back a smile when he finally made it to the flap and stepped outside. He obviously felt guilty or he wouldn't be trying so hard not to repeat his mistake.

While he was gone, I took stock of my life. The past few days had been traumatic. I'd lost track of how long I was out there in the forest, but it was at least three days. Maybe more. Sometimes the trees had been so thick, it had been hard to see if it was light or dark out. I hadn't stopped to sleep often, only when I couldn't keep going, so I couldn't use that to track the passing of time. Was I now far enough away that they couldn't find me anymore? Or would they show up here like Finn's brother, demanding my return so they could deal with me properly? That was a terrifying thought.

Unfortunately, there was nothing I could do about that currently. I would be unable to move on my own for who knew how long, so I was stuck with a barbarian clan that I knew nothing about and who spoke a different language. I'd been told more than once that I was safe, but after everything that had happened, it was hard to trust that. Even if they weren't lying, and I was allowed to stay, how long would that last? Would they demand something in return? I could work once I could walk on my own, but would they even need me? Was it better to leave now?

The barbarian came back while I was still trying to figure out what to do. Everything was a mess, and my heart ached for what I'd lost. I didn't even get to tell my family. Did they know what had happened to me? Did they even care?

"Ravsol," the barbarian called gently, drawing my attention. I frowned to show I didn't know what that meant, but he didn't explain it to me. He sat cross-legged next to my bed, a bowl of food in his lap. My stomach rumbled again as the smell of smoked meats, fresh bread, and herbs hit my nose.

He offered me the food, but when my hands trembled, he took the bowl back with a frown, instead tearing little pieces for me so I could hold them easier. It was thoughtful and sweet, and it helped a lot to get food in me quickly, which I appreciated. I was too hungry to eat slowly but too weak to eat quickly on my own. And the barbarian determined to protect me didn't complain once, patiently feeding me until I felt full for the first time in days, and the exhaustion dragged at my senses again. He put his hand on my forehead, whispering to me in a soothing tone. I drifted off, thinking maybe, for right now, I could just stay and feel safe for a little while. At least until I was strong enough to move on my own. Would it really be so bad?

Six

Rath was right. Moving slowly helped a lot. The male let me care for him as long as I moved slowly. I fed him and helped him drink, and sat beside him while he slept to make sure he didn't wake scared and alone. I may have dozed off at one point, but I was used to sleeping in odd positions while on long hunts. Sleeping sitting up wasn't difficult for me. I stretched out the kinks from the position as I woke, letting out a contented sigh when the muscles relaxed. When I opened my eyes, I checked on the male, but he was still asleep. Zoya had put some herbs in his food to help with the pain and help him to sleep. She said he needed lots of rest to heal.

Since he seemed quite hungry the night before, I figured getting him food was best. I carefully snuck out of the healer's tent, bumping into Zoya as she tried to come in. I caught her arms to prevent her from tripping, checking her over once she was stable on her feet.

"Are you well?" I whispered.

She looked amused, resting her hand on her belly absentmindedly. "Yes, I'm fine. Why are you whispering?"

I pointed behind me and kept my voice low. "The male is still asleep. I am going to get him breakfast. Is there anything he needs?"

She looked thoughtful, her head tipped in that sweet way it always did when she was thinking. I loved Zoya like a sister. She cared for a lot of my injuries after hunting. Including the scratches from the shadowstalker, which were wrapped still but no longer tender.

"Meat is good. And a variety of fruits and vegetables. Nothing too special."

"Have you eaten? I can bring you some too," I offered, since she was pregnant and needed to eat.

She smiled at me. "I ate, but I'm always hungry now. Some bread and fruit would be nice. Thank you, Verus."

Nodding, I hurried off to grab their food, making a detour along the way to relieve myself and splash cool water from the river on my face. I liked to wake myself up in such a way, as did many of my brothers. I got a few greetings from brothers who were awake, but most were still asleep so early. There was only one who was guaranteed to be awake at this hour. Ducking into the cooking tent, I gave Yamileth a bright smile.

"Good morning, sweet Yamileth. How are you?"

She scowled at me, as was her nature. She was growing older, and needed more help to feed the village, but she trusted no one to assist her. All who volunteered felt her wrath as she barked orders at them all day. It had become a challenge throughout the clan to see who could get her to smile. It only counted if she did so at a clan meeting or ceremony where all could see her, otherwise I would have won already. She liked me more than the rest, because while I was hunting, I picked herbs along the way and brought them back without her having to wait for another to get around to it.

"Did you get me hyath like I asked?" she demanded, hand already outstretched. I had managed to find a little and gave her what I had, but when she frowned at me, I hurried to explain why it wasn't more.

"I found a male in the forest on my last hunt. He was being attacked by a shadowstalker. He was injured and needed to see Zoya quickly, so my hunt was cut short before I could find more."

Yamileth was a surly woman by nature, but she cared deeply for the injured and took great care with their meals. They were always served first, along with mothers with new babes. None in the clan minded the arrangement.

"What does Zoya recommend for him?"

I knew she'd ask, which was why I'd asked Zoya before I left. "Meat. And a variety of fruits and vegetables for his health, she said. I also am grabbing her some bread and fruit, since her babe makes her hungry."

Yamileth huffed, puttering over to the pot she already had over the fire. "Of course, she's hungry. She's growing one of you. Only the strongest can do such things. You would not be able to handle it."

Yamileth had three sons. All warriors for our clan. All as large as Rath. She was truly a brave woman. I kissed the top of her head when she handed me a platter with what I needed, grinning when she blushed and scowled. She might be older, but she still blushed with male attention. Before he died, her bondmate would tease her constantly to make her cheeks turn that color. He said it brought out her eyes.

"I am grateful to you, dearest Yamileth. You are a treasure to our clan."

"Oh, stop that. I put in enough for you as well. Now get moving. I have a clan to feed."

She truly was the greatest. She could have easily made me wait until the rest of the clan was awake and ready to eat. She spoiled me because she said I reminded her of her bondmate.

When I came back to the healing tent, the male was awake and propped up with some cushions. He was sipping water, his hands much steadier than they had been the night prior. I only admitted to myself that I was disappointed. I liked the excuse of holding his hands while helping him.

"You've returned unscathed," Zoya said with a smile as she ground some healing herbs in a bowl. "Is Yamileth in a good mood today?"

I lifted a shoulder. "She has a new charge to feed. She will no doubt be visiting after the meal is through to make sure he is full and happy."

She hummed, smiling at me, before turning to repeat what we said to the male. I sat down next to him because I could not resist, and when he flashed me a small smile, I felt as though I could triumph in all things. I settled the platter between us, beckoning Zoya to join us so she could feed her babe.

The male asked a question, pointing at the food, and she answered him readily before looking at me. "You want to be his protector so bad, you should start teaching him the language. He will feel better once he can understand everyone's words."

I nodded in agreement before frowning. "How… do I do that exactly?"

She pursed her lips as though she was fighting back a laugh. I did my best not to scowl at her. She only teased. I just wished caring for the male came as easily for me as it did for Rath.

IT TOOK OVER A WEEK BEFORE THE MALE COULD LEAVE THE HEALING TENT. He was in too much pain to move before that, and Zoya worried about his leg not healing well if he was moved too soon. I technically wasn't his protector yet, since Orthorr hadn't agreed to let me officially take on the role, so I couldn't stay with him the whole time. I had to return to the hunt. I no longer challenged Rath for biggest kill. I got what I could as quickly as I could so I could return to the male's side as soon as possible.

Patrick.

Zoya told me his name after the second day of me calling him 'the male', but I didn't start using it until he told it to me himself. I wanted to hear it from his own mouth to make sure I said it correctly. When I told him my name, he blushed prettily while repeating it, making the spots on his face stand out.

Ducking into the healing tent, I came up short to find Patrick on his feet, wooden supports under his arms so he could better balance on one leg. He still couldn't move the other, and Zoya said it would take weeks before he was able to bear any weight upon it, but it looked as though they were attempting to get him to move on his own.

"What are you doing?"

"They're called crutches," Zoya said, standing worriedly beside Patrick as though she would try to catch him if he fell. That was unsafe. She was pregnant, and he was bigger than her. I moved to take her place, following as he carefully hopped the length of the tent.

"They seem unstable," I grumbled, lunging forward and pulling up short when Patrick wobbled but managed to stay upright.

"Mm. It will take some practice, I think," Zoya murmured, watching

Patrick's progress. "I had Ithrir make them from what I could remember of them, but it's been a while."

When Patrick wobbled a little harder this time, I caught his waist to steady him, frowning at Zoya. "This is not safe. Why can I not just carry him where he needs to go?"

That was what we'd done thus far. Only ever to the trench to relieve himself, but it was not like it was a hardship for me. He wasn't heavy.

"Because you are not his protector, and he needs to be able to move around when you aren't here," Zoya chided, frowning at me.

Straightening, I frowned back. "I am his protector. I found him. I watch out for him. I will keep him safe."

Seven

I wasn't sure either of them was aware I could understand them. Not everything in its entirety, but enough to know why they were arguing. Finn stopped by when Zoya was busy to keep me company, and he spent most of his visits teaching me the language. Apparently, he was writing a book for the clan's language, so it was easier to teach it to tributes when they came to join the clan. The language itself wasn't actually that hard to learn, but he spoke with many of the other tributes, who said it sometimes took months for them to be able to have anything resembling a conversation because some of the barbarians didn't know how to teach a language. Like Verus. He had good intentions, but aside from pointing at things and naming them, he didn't really know how to teach me.

It still surprised me how determined Verus was to be my protector. I thought he'd consider his duties done once I was moving on my own, so I mentioned the crutches to Zoya, but if anything, it only made him more determined to take over my care.

Was it wrong that I was charmed by that?

"He doesn't need a protector. He is not a tribute. He is a visitor who was injured," Zoya snapped, glaring at him. She followed up with a sentence too fast for me to catch, but it made Verus very unhappy.

"He is mine, Zoya," he practically bellowed. When I looked over my shoulder at him, his teeth were bared like they were in the forest the day he rescued me. He looked feral and dangerous, not like the sweet man I'd come to know.

Worried he'd do something crazy like try to kidnap me again, I carefully turned around, wobbling with every movement thanks to my limited grasp on how to use the crutches effectively. My movements at least claimed Verus's attention before he went on a rampage. He didn't normally act this way, so I was confused about why he was so angry now.

When I faced him, Verus looked like he was fighting his emotions. He'd been careful around me since scaring me that first day. He was trying to mask his anger so he didn't frighten me again.

Balancing on my good leg, I reached for him, touching his cheek gently. It pulled his attention down to me, and his face softened little by little. My ability to understand the language was better than my ability to speak it, but I did my best to communicate with him.

"Why angry?"

He shook his head, denying me, so I pushed again. "Why Verus angry?"

He sighed. "Patrick is hurt. I want to help."

Butterflies fluttered in my belly, and while I did my best not to trust those feelings anymore, it didn't stop me from blushing all the way up to my hairline. Finn had warned me that the barbarians were criminally sweet and would win me over. I needed to have better control over my emotions. I wasn't going to stay. I wasn't a tribute. I had no place here.

Since he was so determined to help, I figured a task would distract him enough for me to speak with Zoya alone. I waved a hand at my clothes and winced. "New clothes?"

I was not walking, or hobbling, around the clan in just a tunic. It barely landed mid thigh, and I'd had to beg Finn for my smallclothes back because I didn't like how exposed I was. I couldn't dress like this forever, and I couldn't put my leg in trousers while it was splinted, so I wasn't sure what to do about it.

Verus tipped his head, looking me over before turning to Zoya, his tone gruff but resigned. "He can wear leg coverings?"

She still looked annoyed, but my ploy worked to distract them both.

Verus scooped me up and settled me on the bed while they discussed options for me to cover myself. It still stunned me every time that he moved me around so easily. He acted as though I weighed as little as Finn did.

"Ask Naeth to create something. It has to go over the splint without jostling but still keep him warm."

Verus nodded and stood, taking a step toward the exit before turning around again. "Patrick okay?"

A smile tugged at my lips as I nodded. "I'm okay. See you later."

He looked reluctant but eventually left. Zoya sighed heavily after he stepped out, shaking her head.

Switching to my own language, since it was easier for me, I asked, "What's wrong?"

"Nothing. He's just being stubborn. Since he only knows the process for caring for tributes, he sees no other option. I've lost count of how many conversations I've had with him this week about not moving you to his tent."

"Why would he want to do that?" I asked, alarmed.

She shrugged. "It's just the way things work here. When tributes first arrive, they can't be trusted not to run away. As you well know, it's dangerous in the forest, and I can't tell you how many women got hurt before the clan put a rule in place that tributes stay in their protector's tents until they understand they're safe here and why it's dangerous to leave alone."

"And he wants me to stay with him? It's not like I can run away." I gestured wryly to my leg.

She chuckled, shaking her head. "It's not about that. The tributes usually stay longer with their protectors because they're comfortable with them. The protectors teach them how the clan functions and how important they are. About fifty percent of the time, the protectors also become bondmates to their tributes. You might be trusted not to run, but you still need a lot of care. He wants to take on that responsibility and keep you close. I'm just worried he's going to forget that your stay is only temporary. You weren't heading for us when you were in the forest, were you?"

I shook my head. No one had asked yet why I was in the forest. They saw I needed help and took care of me. That had warmed me a lot to the clan since I arrived.

"Technically, I wasn't running *to* anywhere. I was running away. I'm still worried they're going to show up here and try to force me back so they can punish me properly."

Her eyebrows shot up in surprise. "Did you do something wrong?"

"Who did what wrong?" Finn asked as he slipped into the tent. His cheeks were flushed, and his hair was disheveled. It was still shocking to see such blatant evidence that he was bonded to a man and quite happy with the arrangement.

Zoya waved him over, her eyes still locked on me. "Patrick was telling me how he ended up in that forest alone."

Chewing on my bottom lip, I dropped my gaze to my lap. I didn't want to admit it out loud. But they'd been so kind to me. It felt wrong to keep them in the dark.

"I, uh... I was approached by someone... Another man in town. He was a bully in my youth, and I was surprised when he asked to speak with me alone. He confessed to me that he'd been so cruel all those years because he was in love with me and too scared to admit it. He begged for my forgiveness and told me he wanted a relationship with me. I was so starved for affection, I agreed with him and let him convince me to—" I swallowed hard around the embarrassment, tears pricking my eyes. "To use my mouth on him..." Shame made it impossible to look up, and I spat out the rest as quickly as I could. "After he'd finished, his friends showed up saying it was all a ruse. They wanted to stage it like I'd gotten him drunk and assaulted him. I got scared. So I ran. I should've known better. He's always hated me. I was an idiot and—"

"Why is Patrick crying?"

Verus's growl made me jump. I hadn't heard him enter over the pounding of my heart in my ears. I panicked, shrinking in on myself, worried that Finn or Zoya would tell him my shame, but he didn't demand again. Instead, he scooped me up carefully and sat in my place, cradling me against his chest as he petted my hair. The freely given affection tore me apart after admitting what I'd done to even get a scrap of attention. I sobbed against his chest until my lungs burned and my eyes felt swollen.

He shushed me gently, like a mother would her babe, and when I quieted a little, he hummed a little tune to soothe me.

At some point while I was crying, someone propped my injured leg on some cushions to make me more comfortable in Verus's lap. I stayed that way for who knew how long until the ache in my heart settled into something manageable. Not once did Verus complain that I was heavy or a sissy for crying like a girl. I'd spent years learning to hide my emotions and come off more manly, but it just wasn't who I was. And he seemed okay with that.

When I started to nod off, Verus moved to lay me back down on my bed. I clutched harder at his tunic when he tried to pull away.

"Please don't go."

I'd said it in my own language, too exhausted to attempt to translate, but he seemed to understand. His expression softened, and he settled beside me on the opposite side of my injured leg, humming and stroking my hair until I fell asleep cuddled against him.

Why couldn't I have found a man like him before any of this happened? I would have gladly volunteered as a tribute if I knew Verus was waiting for me on the other side.

Eight

I hadn't forgotten my argument with Zoya. I was tired of defending my position as Patrick's protector. I thought only to check on him before going to speak with Orthorr again, but when I found him crying, I could not make myself go. Even after he'd fallen asleep, I didn't move. His hand was fisted in my tunic, keeping me close, his head resting on my arm. He could not cuddle, not with the injury, but it was obvious he needed to be held. I was not taking that from him, and I wouldn't allow anyone else to pull me from him, either.

While he cried, Finn and Zoya stepped out to give him privacy to feel his feelings. I still didn't know what upset him so much, but it didn't really matter. He would tell me when he was ready. Or when he had the ability. He'd surprised me earlier by speaking to me. I hadn't known he could converse so well already.

Finn came back while Patrick slept. He spent a lot of time sitting with members of the clan, writing down our stories. We shared our history through our stories but had never written them down before. Finn was good with words and writing. He volunteered to write it all down for us, and Orthorr was pleased to accept. That Finn was making time to check in with Patrick and teach him the language made me appreciate him even more.

"You have been teaching him," I murmured, quiet enough not to disturb Patrick.

Finn nodded. "He wants to understand. It makes him feel better. He's still scared."

My hold on Patrick tightened a little. "Why? What makes him afraid?" Dread settled into my gut. "It is not me, is it?"

I tried so hard to be calm around him. I got frustrated during my argument with Zoya. I didn't want to scare him.

Thankfully, Finn shook his head with a smile. "No. Not you. When he speaks of you, it is with fond exasperation. You are a bad teacher."

My mouth twisted to hide my smile. That wasn't a terrible assessment. I wasn't sure how to teach our tongue. I pointed out things and told him the words, but I didn't know where else to go with such things.

"I am grateful to you for teaching him."

He patted the leather-bound book in his lap that Rath acquired for him from another clan. "It's what I'm hoping to do for the rest when they come. To help them understand. He's kind to let me practice with him."

They practiced with each other. Finn with his teaching, Patrick with his learning. I hoped they became good friends. It would be one more reason for Patrick to stay.

"What is he afraid of?"

Finn's brow furrowed a little. "I will not tell the story. It is not mine to tell. But he is afraid his town will look for him. They want to hurt him."

Outrage filled me, and it took great work to not crush Patrick against my chest protectively. "For what reason?"

Finn looked resigned when he said, "For being like me. For being attracted to males. It is not allowed in most towns. If they catch you, they'll kill you for it."

I'd heard this from Finn before. He'd had trouble believing such things were of no consequence here. Especially since a tribute from another town was shaming him for it. It took time for him to accept he was free to love who he wished. He chose Rath.

My gaze dropped to Patrick again. I wanted him to choose me. I did not know him well, Zoya refused to translate all day, but he was sweet. He noticed early that I preferred the dark meat on the platter and would put it closer to me so that I could enjoy it. His eyes, dark green like the forest I loved so much, were always soft, full of what I hoped was affection. I wanted to keep him, to bond with him, but many continued to remind me he would not stay forever. Once he was healed, he would leave. And my heart would go with him.

"You like him," Finn murmured.

I hummed and did not bother to deny it. "He calls to me."

"Oh. You want to bond with him?" He sounded surprised, drawing my attention off of Patrick's sweet face. "I thought it was only temporary."

"Would he choose me, I would not say no. But it is not my choice to make. You know this."

Finn looked as though he would start crying with my response, startling me.

"What's wrong? What did I say?"

He wiped a stray tear, shaking his head. "It's nothing. You are just very sweet. All of you are. I wonder who started those awful rumors about you. If people knew just how sweet you all are, I'm sure they would be clamoring to join you."

The idea made me smile, but I shook my head. I did not believe that. It was not only our clan that had tributes, and not all were like us. It was because of them that the rumors existed. We did not deal with them often, but the few clan wars we had were with them. I would not tell Finn this, though. He was a gentle soul, and I did not want to frighten him.

He stayed for a while, keeping me company while I lay with Patrick. After a time, Patrick's grip on me loosened as he fully relaxed, but I could not make myself move from him, and thankfully, no one asked me to. It was only when Rath returned from the hunt that Finn left.

"Verus."

I looked up at Finn in the entrance to the tent. He looked soft and full of affection. I wasn't sure what I'd done to earn that look.

"Hmm?"

"You are his protector. He feels safe with you. He wouldn't cling to you otherwise. If he wants to stay, I hope he chooses you, too."

My heart ached for it, but I chose not to repeat it. I was not the one who chose. It was up to Patrick if he thought I was worth staying for.

It was late when I woke up with Verus pressed up against my side. I'd slept a lot longer than I thought I would. The fire in the center of the tent was tempered, not so overwhelming but still warm. Even if it was out, I would probably still be plenty warm, thanks to Verus's presence next to me. He was asleep, his forehead resting against mine, his arm not being used as a pillow thrown across my waist.

I shut my eyes for a moment, soaking it in. I was being held by a handsome man who cared for me, and there wasn't any lingering fear that we would be caught and killed for it. Finn assured me more than once that being attracted to men was fine here. He would know, being bonded to one. I wished I could keep things like they were forever. But they liked to remind me I wouldn't be here for very long. I shouldn't get used to being held like this.

My breath stuttered as I fought the urge to cry. Why did everything have to be so grim? Why couldn't I just be happy for once? I'd thought I had that, for just a split second, when Richard confessed to me. It hurt that he gave me that moment, only to rip it away from me again. I couldn't stomach feeling that way twice, but I didn't want to end up alone, either.

Verus's hand moved from my waist to cup my cheek, his thumb stroking over the skin. My eyes flew open in surprise, and I sucked in a sharp breath when I remembered how close he was.

"Why is Patrick sad?"

I shook my head. I didn't want to explain. I didn't want him to remind me again that I couldn't stay.

"I want to make you happy," he murmured, his brow drawing tightly together. "How can I make you happy, Ravsol?"

He'd called me that before. I still didn't know what it meant. It didn't really matter right now. He was offering me happiness and for just one moment, I wanted to seize it. To give myself a better experience than what Richard had done to me.

"Can... Can you kiss me?"

Verus sucked in a breath, and I squeezed my eyes shut, preparing myself for the rejection. I didn't see it coming when he pressed his lips against mine. So soft and slow, like the first day after he scared me when he would creep through every motion to not frighten me again. I couldn't easily chase after him when he pulled away, so I pulled him back down with a gentle grasp on his neck. He groaned into the next kiss, wrapping himself around me, surrounding me with him. I threw my arms around his neck, sinking into the kiss with abandon.

It was... perfect.

Everything I ever dreamed of.

I never ever wanted to stop.

Couldn't I have this forever?

Nine

I lost track of time kissing Verus. He didn't rush or pull away. Didn't shove his tongue into my mouth like I'd seen some couples do. He sipped at my lips until my belly quivered and I broke away with a gasp, only to come back for more because I couldn't get enough. In all my fantasies, I never thought it'd be as all-consuming as this. Just the feel of his lips against mine. I felt like I would float away if he wasn't holding me so tight.

Despite the innocence of the act, my body throbbed with need, and I shifted restlessly against the bedding, flinching when I tried to move my injured leg. That was what drew Verus to stop. He lifted his head, frowning down at my leg before turning back to me.

"We should not continue. You are hurting."

"No," I pleaded, tears filling my eyes. I didn't want to stop. I didn't know if I'd ever experience such pure joy again. "Please."

Verus's smile made my heart skip a beat, and he gave me one more gentle kiss before pulling away completely. "I will deny you nothing, my ravsol, but I will ask you to wait until you are well. I do not wish to hurt you."

"But that could take weeks," I protested. Zoya wasn't sure just how long it would take for my leg to heal. Only that it would take time. It was why she'd had the crutches made for me. So I wouldn't be trapped in this tent for weeks on end.

"Then I will stay by your side until you are ready for more."

His gentle reassurance gave me hope. Maybe I wouldn't be cursed to be alone after all.

∼

It took another few days of practice, and some readjustments to the crutches, but eventually, I could move on my own and leave the healing tent. Which, of course, was when Verus insisted I move in with him instead. It almost started another argument with Zoya until I assured her I was happy to do it. Verus had slept beside me every night in the healing tent since I cried in his arms. I'd grown to crave it, and I wondered if I'd ever be able to sleep well without him. He was so warm.

My agreement to stay with him put Verus in a very good mood. He strutted around like a rooster, a big grin on his face, until some of his friends started teasing him. I watched him from my spot on the cushions next to Finn. I couldn't go far yet without getting tired, but the healing tent was near the village center, where a massive fire blazed throughout the day to promote feelings of warmth and welcome. It was where many craftspeople worked on their craft so they could socialize and make trades. Finn told me everyone was seen as equal because one position could not thrive without the rest to support them. It was fascinating to me.

"He looks happy," Finn commented when he looked up from his book. Not his work today, he was taking the day for himself to rest at his bondmate's request. Rath said he was working too hard. He bought Finn books through clan trades, which made his bookworm bondmate unbelievably happy. It was cute to watch Finn gush over the moment.

"This morning, I told him I would stay with him in his tent," I admitted quietly. I still wasn't used to speaking so openly about my interests in a man.

Finn's head jerked around, and he beamed brightly. "Really?"

I felt my face flame as I nodded. It felt a little like I was admitting to being intimate with the barbarian. We hadn't; Verus said we couldn't do anything besides kiss until I was better. But that didn't mean I didn't want to.

"Well, no wonder he looks like that, then. He's been wishing for it since the day you showed up."

I knew that, but it still made me smile. He went about it in all the wrong ways, but he'd shown me the day he saved me in the woods that he wanted me. And now he had me. For as long as he wanted to keep me.

A familiar face appeared out of one of the tents, and I braced myself for the fussing. Yamileth was the village cook. She visited a lot when I was in the healing tent, to make sure I was getting everything I needed to heal. She basically adopted me, making me special meals and checking on me often. I never knew that kind of affection, my parents weren't overly affectionate themselves when I was younger, and I floundered a little every time she came to see me.

"Verus told me you are moving around now. How do you feel?" she demanded when she stepped up to me. She immediately touched my face, checking me over. I felt my cheeks flush from the warm gesture.

"I'm okay. A little slow. It is not easy." My sentences were all simple, but Finn said I was learning quickly, and at least I could follow most conversations now. He was a good teacher.

She eyed the crutches and made a face. "No. I imagine it is difficult. Rest often. You are well enough to leave the healing tent, but you are not well. You need rest."

"Verus is taking care of him," Finn piped up shyly. He'd been with the clan a few months and knew everyone, but he was still quiet.

Yamileth didn't begrudge him his silence. She just nodded and patted my cheek affectionately before turning to Finn. "I have a request for you, clan scribe."

He sat up a little straighter. "Y-yes?"

"I wish to write down my recipes. I will not live forever, and I do not want them lost. No one here can be trusted to learn them correctly and share them."

I tipped my head with a frown. "No one helps you?"

She scoffed, scowling at the nearby clan members. "They try—and only make more work for me. I worry for what will happen once I am gone."

While Finn nodded and promised her he'd visit her soon to start writing, I considered my options. I wasn't sure it would be a good idea to offer her help if they were just going to send me on my way soon. But it might be a good way for me to pay them back a little for helping me.

"I, uh… I can cook. I can help."

She looked amused by the prospect, looking me over. "How? You struggle to move more than I do. You are supposed to be resting."

I winced. I didn't know how to say the words I needed in their language. I looked to Finn for help. "Can you translate for me? We haven't gone over cooking words yet."

He nodded. "Go ahead."

With Finn translating, I turned back to Yamileth. "While I'm sitting, I can chop and prepare vegetables and meats, knead dough. I had my own bakery, so I'm good at that. You're right that I can't do everything, but I can at least ease some of the burden. And with Finn there taking down recipes, I'll still be learning the language too."

They both seemed happy with the offer, and Yamileth patted my cheek again with obvious affection. "You are a sweet boy. If your protector can figure out a way for you to be comfortable while helping me, I will allow it. But if you hurt, you will stop. Understand?"

I nodded. "I understand. Thank you."

She chuckled, pinching my cheek a little. "You are helping me. I will thank you. Maybe. If you do not cause more work for me. I start before dawn. Your protector should be up by then for the hunt, anyway. Have him bring you to me."

Waking up early wasn't anything new for me. And I looked forward to having something to do to give back to the clan that took such good care of me. After I was hurt, I thought I was doomed. But they were trying so hard to help me and get me back on my feet. I wanted to do everything I could to pay them back.

I waited until we were back in his tent before telling Verus that I volunteered to help Yamileth. He looked curious as he helped me get more comfortable in his bed.

"You can cook?"

I nodded. "I, um… I had…" The word for bakery escaped me. I heard Finn use it while translating, but it didn't stick. "A place where I sold bread in town."

"Bakery," he corrected with a soft smile. "You are getting better."

I flushed at his praise and shrugged. "I want to learn."

My reply seemed to make him happy, and he rewarded me with a sweet kiss that thrilled me to my toes. He offered his affection so easily, without asking for anything in return. When he pulled away, I fisted his tunic with a frown. I didn't want to let go.

"Verus…"

I wished I didn't have to go. I wished I was a tribute like Finn. But all anyone ever reminded me of was the fact that this was all temporary. I hated that. Who knew if I'd be able to find anything close to this anywhere else?

"Whatever you need, ravsol. It is yours."

The words were there. I just couldn't get them out of my mouth. I didn't want to burden him. I doubted there was anything he could do about it. I just had to soak up as much of him as I could get before they sent me away.

"I want… you."

Ten

I was nervous. The last time I fooled around with someone, everything went wrong in the worst ways. But I also didn't want to risk losing what little time with Verus that I had. I trusted him not to be cruel like Richard was. And if I did have to go, at least I'd have the memory of being with Verus to bring with me.

Verus studied my face, like he didn't quite understand my meaning. I held my breath, preparing myself for rejection, but he didn't automatically say no. He did frown, though, cupping my cheeks and resting his forehead against mine.

"I don't want to hurt you," he murmured.

It meant a lot that he cared so much. Richard hadn't been kind. But I wasn't willing to wait until I was fully healed. Once I was, they'd send me away. I had to take the opportunity I could.

"You won't. I trust you."

He looked surprised, and his expression melted into a huge smile. When he leaned down to capture my lips, I got to taste it. It was like sunshine wrapped in a kiss, and I couldn't get enough. I cradled his face in my hands to keep him close, relaxing back into the bedding as he laid me down. My heart thundered in my chest, and I wasn't sure what would happen next, but I trusted Verus. It would be okay.

When his tongue trailed over my bottom lip, I parted my lips on a gasp, arching a little when his tongue dipped in to touch mine. He wasn't in any hurry, slowly tasting me with one hand cupping my cheek. I grew breathless, and I hardened in my trousers, but Verus didn't move until I was squirming and pulling at his tunic impatiently.

Breaking the kiss, he grinned at me. "You must stay still, ravsol. I do not want you hurting."

"I'm okay," I promised. And I was. It still hurt if I moved my leg around or tried to put weight on it, but just lying here, I wasn't in any pain. The splint was strong enough to keep my leg immobile.

Verus hummed, but he didn't look like he fully believed me. He didn't stop, though. He pressed a quick kiss to my lips before trailing a few more along my jaw. I shivered when he kissed just beneath my ear and tipped my head as he trailed farther down my neck. When he sucked lightly on the skin where my neck met my shoulder, tingles spread through my body, and I let out an embarrassing breathy moan.

He lifted his head again to look at me, and I felt my cheeks burn, but he didn't look teasing or judgmental. His gaze was heated, and he looked like he wanted to devour me.

"You make the most beautiful sounds," he murmured, capturing my lips in a fierce kiss before breaking it again. "You make me want to—" He said some things then that I couldn't understand, but I understood the tone. He wasn't whispering sweet nothings to me. He was talking dirty, and I desperately wished I could understand him. The tone alone made me whimper.

At least I could tell he wasn't lying about what he was saying. He groaned in response to my noises, his next kiss a little more frantic as he got riled up. His hands drifted down my body and tugged my tunic free of my trousers. They were looser in the legs, almost like a skirt, to easily fit over my injury and the splint, but they kept me warm and covered. I shivered again when his fingers drifted along the skin of my stomach, biting back a laugh when he got to my side. When I squirmed away from him, he lifted his head, studying me for a second before a wicked grin crossed his face. He wiggled his fingers, tickling my side, and his grin grew when I laughed and squirmed.

"Ah. My Patrick is—" He said another word that I assumed meant ticklish because his smile was a little too smug for me. He was going to use that information against me.

To distract him, I fisted his tunic and yanked him into another kiss, daring myself to push my tongue into his mouth. He groaned in response, forgetting all about the tickling as he kissed me back. When his hands moved again, it was to pull off my tunic and toss it out of the way.

I helped him with his, eager to get my hands on his skin. He cuddled me plenty, but never shirtless. I wanted to feel his skin against mine.

Sucking in a sharp breath, I took in all the ridges and dips. There wasn't an ounce of fat on him. He wasn't as wide as some of the other barbarians, but he was just as muscled, and I'd seen him fight. He was easily their equal, despite the small size difference. And he was still a lot bigger than me. It made me a little embarrassed, actually, since I was as soft as he was muscled. Too much bread for my meals, maybe. I felt my cheeks pinken so harshly it spread down my neck and into my chest.

If Verus noticed my embarrassment, he didn't point it out. He started trailing kisses over me again, this time past my neck and to my chest. When his tongue flicked over my nipple, I forgot all about my embarrassment, gasping as lightning shot straight to my groin.

"Verus..." I breathed.

He hummed to acknowledge me but didn't pull his focus off my chest. I never realized I was so sensitive, but it took very little attention from him before I felt close to coming in my trousers.

"Verus, please," I murmured, squirming a little more. My cock was leaking heavily and throbbed with each suction of his mouth. I couldn't take much more.

He pulled away slowly, looking at me with pure lust in his eyes. It was so different from the way Richard had looked at me. I felt foolish now seeing the difference. The hint of malice that had made me so hesitant was gone. Only affection and adoration stood out in Verus's eyes. It made my stomach quiver and my heart clench. I hoped he'd always look at me this way.

He had to stand to remove his trousers. My mouth fell open when he straightened.

"Goddess…" I murmured, staring at him. His erection was long and thick, standing proudly out from his body. He wrapped his fingers around it, stroking a few times, and I bit my lip, trying to hold back the needy noises that wanted to escape me. He was beautiful.

"I like the way you look at me," he said, a crooked grin on his lips. He sank to his knees beside me, leaning over me for another kiss. It put him close to me, and I couldn't resist reaching out to touch. I brushed my fingers down his length, trailing over the veins down to his balls. He shuddered and shifted closer, his expression tight as he let me explore him. He wasn't in any rush like Richard had been, even though I could tell he wanted more. A drop of precum beaded on his tip, and when my thumb brushed over it, spreading it down his length, he groaned outright.

"Patrick," he murmured, his voice like a plea.

My stomach clenched, and a flash of the experience I'd had with Richard made me back away slightly. I liked touching Verus, but… I wasn't ready to take him into my mouth. He was much larger than Richard had been. I was worried it would hurt.

I didn't want to disappoint him, though. He was so kind to me, and it was my idea to ask for more. Maybe he wasn't wrong to have asked to wait.

My hand had frozen in my turmoil, and Verus definitely noticed. He tipped his head, his expression concerned.

"What's wrong?"

I couldn't explain. I didn't have the words to, even if I had the nerve. I shook my head helplessly.

Verus didn't look angry with me. His expression softened, and he leaned to kiss my forehead before speaking again, slowly, so he was sure I could understand him.

"Finn said interest in men isn't allowed in towns. You are allowed to have fears because of this. You are safe here, my Patrick. I will keep you safe."

He kissed me again, soothing my insecurities. It wasn't exactly why I was so nervous, but a small part of me did worry about it sometimes. Seeing Finn cuddled with his bondmate when we were eating with the clan helped a lot. And I saw a few warriors sitting too close to be considered just friendly. It really was accepted here. I didn't need to worry about that. I didn't need to worry about pain either. Verus had been determined to protect and take care of me since the day I showed up here. He wouldn't hurt me.

When I nodded, Verus smiled at me, making butterflies explode through my stomach. He truly was the most beautiful man I'd ever met. He kept me distracted with little kisses, like the ones he gave me the first time I asked for intimacy from him. They still made me breathless and so unbelievably happy I couldn't help but smile. While I was distracted, Verus undid the ties on my trousers and slipped them down my hips, careful not to jostle my injured leg, slowing his trailing kiss to remove them completely.

It was hard not to compare my body to his. He was all tight, compact lines, and I was—

"You are so beautiful," Verus breathed, interrupting my worrying thoughts. I jerked my gaze to his, surprised.

"You—You think I'm beautiful?"

His gaze trailed over me, and I couldn't see any hint of disgust or disinterest. He looked at me like I was something precious. I couldn't help it then, falling a little bit in love with him. If he kept looking at me like that, I'd never leave his side.

Eleven

I could tell Patrick was nervous. I assumed him untouched, like Finn had been. If it was illegal in towns to be with another male, it would have been dangerous to have even a quick tryst. If he was inexperienced like I assumed, the nerves were expected. I decided to take it slow for now. He could explore when he was more sure of me and my intentions. I liked the idea of taking my time with him.

Wrapping my fingers around him, I bit back a groan when he let out a startled gasp, thrusting into my hand. He was new to this. I would not do well to get too excited by his reactions. I did not want this to be over too soon. I was supposed to be his teacher.

"Try not to move," I encouraged. "You will hurt yourself."

His injury still worried me, but right now, Patrick didn't seem to notice it. He reached for me, drawing me into another sweet kiss, and moaned prettily against my lips when I stroked him again.

His length, only slightly smaller than mine, leaked heavily from the tip. My mouth watered to taste him, but he wouldn't release my lips long enough to let me. He peppered me with needy kisses, and I happily responded to each one. I could spend all night kissing Patrick. I couldn't keep him up late, though. He was to help Yamileth in the morning. I was eager for him to find a place here so that maybe he would change his mind and wish to stay. Finding work that made him happy would help with that.

His hips rose as he began to thrust into my hand. I loved his eagerness but worried about his injury. To spare him more pain and keep him still, I moved to straddle his hips. When my cock brushed along his, he cried out a little needy sound, and my control nearly broke. His noises were too sweet.

Wrapping my fist around the both of us, I stroked just once, testing the waters. Patrick's mouth fell open, his breath coming out in heavy pants as he tried to thrust into my hand again. With my position, it was harder for him. Which was good, because if he joined in too much, I would embarrass myself. It was better that I could just focus on him.

"Be at ease, my ravsol. I will take care of you."

I gave a few strokes of our lengths together, watching Patrick's lashes flutter as he moaned and writhed. One of his hands clutched my thigh, like he needed the touch to steady him. I liked him touching me, and I would happily let him do as he wished if it made him feel good. It would feel better with some oil, though, so I leaned away for a moment, snagging the jar from my chest nearby. I poured a little onto my palm, slicking up my cock before doing the same for Patrick. He cried out, his fingers digging a little rougher into my thigh as he writhed in pleasure. I cursed under my breath. I needed to move this along. I couldn't take much more.

Wrapping my oil-slicked hand around us both, I stroked again, my own breath stuttering in my chest as pleasure coiled in my belly. Patrick's length against mine, both silky soft and hard as rock, was the stuff of dreams. I quickly lost what little control I had, stroking us faster as I raced towards my release.

Forcing my eyes open, and questioning when I'd closed them, I locked my gaze on Patrick. I wanted to watch him experience this pleasure we shared. And he was so beautiful to watch. His lips, swollen from my many kisses, were parted as he gasped and moaned, his eyes squeezing shut and opening again immediately, like he too didn't want to look away. His gaze flicked from my face to my hand as I worked us over, and when I squeezed gently, his back arched off the bedding.

"Verus!"

His cry cut out as his body went taut. His length throbbed against mine as he exploded, covering his chest and belly with his release. The image proved to be too much, and I came with a shout a moment later, jerking us rapidly to draw out our pleasure until I was too sensitive and had to let go.

Careful not to collapse on top of him, I rolled to his good side instead, panting as I tried to catch my breath. I'd had sex before, plenty of times. None of those experiences even came close to what it felt like to be with Patrick. He truly was my perfect match.

∼

PATRICK FELL ASLEEP NOT LONG AFTER, AND I WAS HAPPY TO CLEAN HIM UP myself. I liked taking care of him. And he seemed receptive to it, smiling and blushing whenever I did. Even in his sleep, he hummed a happy sound and curled as much as he could into my side without moving his injured leg. I drifted off with a smile on my face.

Sometime in the night, I woke to Patrick whimpering in his sleep. Not the good kind of whimpering he made when I touched him. This sound was laced with terror, and his whole body was tight. He had sweat along his temples and his breathing came out too fast for sleep. I wanted to wake him from whatever dream he was having, but I didn't want to scare him. Carefully, I pulled him into my arms, whispering in his ear.

"Patrick… Ravsol, wake up."

He didn't hear me at first. He kept jerking, like he was trying to get away from the dreams and wake himself up. I had to whisper his name a few times to get him to finally open his eyes. He sucked in a sharp breath, nearly bolting upright. Only my hold on him kept him from getting up.

"Shh… You're alright. You're with me. You're safe."

He let out a muffled sob, burying his face against me. His whole body shook from fear. I rubbed his back, giving him time to wake fully and let the nightmare pass. I hummed a tune my mother used to sing to me before her passing. It always made me feel better when I was upset or scared.

Patrick settled after a few moments, and when he finally spoke, he sounded more like himself. "That's pretty. What is it?"

"A song my mother used to sing to me," I explained, pressing a kiss to the top of his head. I didn't want to leave him in this position for long. It no doubt hurt his leg to lie on his side like this. But I wasn't letting him go until he asked me to or I felt like he was better.

"Like a lullaby?" he asked.

When he snuggled in a little closer as much as we were able without him fulling turning on his side, I tightened my grip on him until we were pressed together from shoulder to hip, my forehead resting against his so he could feel my care for him.

I hummed an agreement. "Yes. Not many know it. She was from a town far from here. The language spoken was different from the common tongue. It took her longer to learn our words because of it."

She was a surprise to my father when he became her protector. Fearful at first, as most tributes were, but when she finally felt safe and secure, her personality shone through and made the whole clan smile. She was playful and teasing, and she charmed my father before she was even introduced to the clan. He introduced her because he was an honorable man, but he growled and snapped at anyone who got too close. In the end, his brothers respected his claim, and they were bonded a few days later. Their time together was short before her passing but full of light and happiness.

It was still dark, so I'd hoped Patrick wouldn't notice the change in my mood, but he was more perceptive than I thought because he asked, "What happened to her?"

I sighed, my heart aching at the memory. "She got sick. Our healers did everything they could for her, but..."

My father and I ended up going on a journey with her to bring her back to her hometown. It gave her a chance to see her family one last time. One day, she woke up with more energy than usual and asked us to take her to the beach. I thought maybe being home was helping, and she'd get better. Instead, she died in my father's arms on that beach just as the sun was setting.

The pain rolled through me like it had happened days ago, not years. It always did when I thought too hard about her. My father never recovered from her loss. He joined Rath's parents when they went to help another clan after I became a man. We didn't see each other often. I think I reminded him too much of her.

Patrick's warm hand slid around the back of my neck, pulling me closer until my face was buried against his shoulder. I sucked in a shaking breath, soaking up the comfort he offered, and wrapped myself around him. He was everything I needed when my heart hurt too much, his presence and warmth like a balm to my soul. I knew then that if Patrick was determined to move on, I would go with him. I couldn't not. I needed him.

Twelve

After years of working in a bakery, I always woke up early, and Verus was never far behind me. He was back to his normal bouncy self, smiling at me as he carried me to the river to wash my face. I could walk on my own with the crutches, but he always waved off any attempt to suggest it. After several days of this routine, I stopped asking. I liked being held by him enough that I didn't want to give it up.

Memories of the way his voice trembled as he spoke about his mother a few nights prior, and the tight hold he had on me afterward, flooded my mind as he gently set me down. He was hiding a lot of pain behind that smile. How many people even knew he was suffering? I could easily hear the heartache and tension that had laced his tone. It hurt my heart to hear it, but at the same time, I felt glad that he was so willingly vulnerable with me. He really was Richard's opposite.

I vowed then to stop comparing the two. Verus was not Richard. They shared absolutely no similarities, and it would do me no good to constantly worry about it. I wanted to soak up all the time I had with Verus while I could, not waste it on thoughts of the cruel man who'd hurt me.

"Will you hunt again today?" I asked Verus as he sat me on a log near the river's edge. It was a convenient spot for me to sit while I got cleaned up. If I sat sideways with my injured leg on the log, then I felt no pain at all.

Verus hummed and nodded. "Yes. We do most every day. There are many mouths to feed. I will try my best not to be gone from you for too long, though."

His sweet words made my heart swell, and I felt myself blush because of it. I wished I could thank Verus's mother for making him. He was a true gift.

Every time he left to hunt, I remembered how dangerous the forest was, and my heart stuttered a little. When he came closer to pick me up again, I put my hands on his cheeks, resting my forehead against his. "Please be careful. It's dangerous out there. I don't want you to get hurt."

He smiled softly at me. "I will be safe, my ravsol. I will ensure I come back to you."

He dipped his head for a kiss, and I greedily returned it, wrapping my arms around his neck to keep him close. He didn't seem in any rush to end it, which made me unbearably happy. It'd been a few days since we were first intimate, and he still seemed eager to kiss me every morning. He kneeled beside me, wrapping one arm around me, and brought the other hand to cup my face, his thumb stroking against my cheek. I was so distracted by him, I didn't hear the footsteps approaching until voices spoke behind us.

"I should have guessed Verus would seduce the male as soon as he could get his hands on him. He has always been a scoundrel," someone teased.

"You're just jealous that he has yet to give his affections to you," someone else replied.

I pulled away on instinct, apprehensive of the tones of their voices. I never did trust teasing. There was always cruelty hidden underneath it.

Verus didn't look happy about the interruption, either. He glared over his shoulder, keeping me close and mostly hidden by his body. I peeked around him at the two barbarians who stood nearby. One was shaped like an upside-down triangle, all brawn. The other was slimmer, more lithe, but his muscles were easily seen along his arms. They had grins that bordered on a sneer, and towels tossed over their shoulders. The upside-down triangle jerked his chin in my direction.

"Getting your fun while you can before he leaves, brother?"

My heart sank at the implication. That wasn't what this was... was it?

Verus growled, releasing me to stand and face the two newcomers. He said something too quick for me to understand, but it made the upside-down triangle's smile fall, his disgust evident.

"Him? You would sink so low as to claim a cow?"

I'd heard the insult before. It wasn't anything new. It still hurt down to my core to hear it. I dropped my gaze to the river bed, wishing I had brought my crutches along so I could leave this place. I needed to join Yamileth. At least there, I could focus on work to hide the pain their words caused.

"Insult my ravsol again, Tavik, and it will be the last thing you do," Verus hissed.

Tavik lifted his chin, sneer on full display now. "He is not a tribute. I can say as I wish. If you want to fight me on it, I will fight back."

That made me nervous. Tavik was bigger than Verus, both in height and in width. The barbarian looked like he could crush someone's head in one hand easily. I didn't want Verus fighting him. He would get hurt.

Reaching for Verus, I tugged gently on his trousers to get his attention. He glanced away from the other two, looking down at me, but his expression was still dark. He was angry, and it was all because of me.

"I... I have to meet Yamileth. I didn't bring my crutches with me."

Verus's jaw flexed, obviously unhappy about not taking the challenge Tavik offered, but he didn't argue with me. Carefully, he plucked me off the log and into his arms, hugging me as tightly to his chest as he could without hurting me. His glare was menacing as he stormed past the other two, but he did not speak to them again. They did not offer the same courtesy.

Once he was far enough away, the other barbarian said, "Verus will be as muscled as you are once that one goes on his way."

Tavik snorted. "Carrying around that amount of weight? He will certainly get a workout."

I hadn't been willing to speak during the walk to meet Yamileth. We stopped in Verus's tent to grab my crutches, and I refused to let Verus carry me again. I could tell it hurt him, but I was too embarrassed to face him. I moved as quickly as I was able to the cooking tent and kept my eyes on the ground as Verus took his leave to hunt. He kissed the top of my head, whispering something to me, but I couldn't hear him over the pounding of my heart in my ears. Tears burned my eyes when he walked away, but I fought them back, sucking in a shaking breath.

"What happened?" Yamileth demanded.

When I glanced over my shoulder at her, she had her arms crossed over her chest and she was frowning so deeply, it pulled at the wrinkles in her face.

I shook my head. "Nothing. Where would you like me to start today?"

She scoffed. "Nothing. Nothing he says. The happiest member of our clan looks murderous, and the man he has been fawning over looks close to tears, and he says nothing." She jabbed a gnarled finger towards a table off to one side. "Go prepare the bread."

I was grateful for the mindless task. I did it most mornings, taking the stool she had set out for me. It was a little harder to do it while sitting, but I made it work, and eventually lost myself in the task, my head clearing enough for me to think. They were words I'd heard before. I did not need to take them to heart.

It's just… those words had never been said in front of my lover before. It was hard enough already being so soft compared to the rest of them. I knew I was fat. My exercise was kneading dough and moving around my shop. I was probably never going to be trim and muscled like Verus. I had accepted that, but I couldn't bear Verus thinking of me that way. What if he was only telling me what I wanted to hear when we lay together the other night? I was not beautiful. I never would be.

A warm hand, tanned and wrinkled with age, stilled mine, pulling me away from the now over-kneaded dough. I sucked in a shaky breath, looking up at Yamileth with tears in my eyes.

"I'm sorry. I didn't mean to—"

She shook her head, stalling me. "I've lost count over the years of the number of times I have taken my anger out on the dough. Sometimes it helps. Others, it doesn't. But holding it all in will only make the hurt fester. So no more saying it's nothing. What happened, young one?"

My bottom lip quivered, but she was right. I was too worked up to help, and I wouldn't settle unless I spoke to someone about it. "Someone... Someone made comments about me that hurt me. I know better than to listen, I've heard those things all my life, but... Verus was there with me and—" I choked on a sob, dropping my gaze to my lap. "I don't want him to think of me that way. It's the truth, but I liked the way he thought of me, and I wanted it not to be a lie. I'm sorry, I shouldn't have overworked the dough. I promised I wouldn't make more work for you."

She hummed. "And what was it that they said that hurt you?"

Her voice sounded stern, and when I looked up at her, she looked almost as angry as Verus had been. She gripped my chin to stop me before I could shake my head more than once.

"None of this. What was said, Patrick?"

With a whimper, I murmured, "They called me a cow. They implied that it was beneath Verus to be with me." I ducked my head when she released my chin, tears escaping and slipping over my cheeks. "I've heard it all before. I know I shouldn't let it get to me. I just..." Wanted to be seen as more. I didn't say that part out loud. It hurt too much. I'd wanted to be different my whole life, skinnier, better looking. More like someone worth loving. It would never happen. I needed to accept it and move on.

"Who said this?" Yamileth demanded, her tone incensed.

I didn't want to tell her. Those men already didn't like me. I didn't want to cause more trouble for the clan by setting Yamileth against them. But when she threatened to take my job away and send me back to Verus's tent to rest until I healed, I panicked and blurted out the name I knew. I wanted to be needed here. It was the only chance I had of being able to stay.

"One was called Tavik. I don't know the other's name," I rushed out.

Yamileth made an irritated sound. "Saneth. Those two are inseparable." Her hands gripped my face again, forcing me to look up at her. "You listen to me, Patrick. You are to pay those two no heed. You are better than them.

And they will regret speaking to you in such a way. Put it from your mind and focus on your work. I will handle the rest."

Eyes wide, I stared up at her. "What do you mean? I don't want to cause trouble. The clan has done a lot for me and—"

She silenced me with a dark look, squeezing my cheeks just rough enough to make me grimace without truly hurting me. "You are no trouble to us, Patrick. You are the only one I trust to help me with the cooking. You bring more to this clan than those two brutes ever will."

The protest must have been clearly written across my face, because she sighed heavily. "I can promise to not bring it to Orthorr unless I absolutely must. Does this settle you?"

Not entirely, but I could see she wouldn't be deterred. Whatever she had planned, it wouldn't go farther than her. How much harm could an old woman truly do?

Thirteen

Rath must have sensed my mood during the hunt, because he did not tease me like usual. He settled onto a branch of the watching tree, speaking low to not startle the creatures of the forest.

"What happened?"

My scowl deepened, but I didn't answer.

The silence stretched between us for a few moments. I wasn't fully present in the hunt. My thoughts strayed constantly to the look on Patrick's face, so full of pain and embarrassment. Tavik's cruel words had hurt him, and if Patrick hadn't asked me to take him to his work, I would have—

"You are growling," Rath pointed out calmly. "Speak now about what bothers you before it scares the entire forest."

I shot him a dirty look. I was not so loud that I would be overheard.

Still, I did not answer him. I could handle Tavik on my own. I didn't need help. I just needed to finish this hunt so I could track him down and hurt him like he hurt Patrick. He would wear his shame for hurting such a sweet man.

"Do you remember when my Finn arrived? He was being harassed but would not seek help. Not even from me. He drew out his suffering by doing this and there was nothing I could do to fix it because I did not have all the information. I asked for your help then, in seeking those who would hurt my bondmate. Why do you not trust me to help you the same way? Have I done something to strain our friendship?"

I grimaced. "No. It is not that. I don't need help to find who hurt Patrick. I know who is responsible. I just didn't have the chance to handle it. Patrick asked me to take him away. I cannot deny him what he wants."

Rath hummed, his eyes constantly scanning the surrounding forest. "That is probably for the best. If he was with you, then getting him somewhere safe should be your first priority. Was his harasser alone?"

The question made me pause. No, Tavik had not been alone. He rarely was. Saneth had been with him. And while most warriors had more honor than to attack an injured man, I didn't trust him. Saneth was in love with Tavik, despite Tavik never returning his affections. Everyone knew this, except maybe Tavik. He would do much to make Tavik happy. Including hurting Patrick while I was distracted with Tavik.

Letting out a slow breath, I nodded. "It was good to get Patrick safely away. I will handle Tavik later."

That made Rath frown, and he swung his gaze to look at me. "Tavik? Why would a clan brother be harassing Patrick?"

"I do not know. He said many cruel things to Patrick, and because Patrick isn't considered a tribute, he feels he can do as he wishes. I will not let him get away with it."

"No, he isn't a tribute, but he is to be your claim, is he not?" Rath asked. The way he said it, like it was already decided, lifted my spirits a little. At least one person was on my side in this.

"I wish him to be," I admitted. "But we have not discussed it. He is recovering and still learning about the clan. He has started helping Yamileth with the cooking, though. I hope that means he wants to stay."

Rath made a disgruntled noise. "It is difficult to read those not from our clan. Learning to read Finn had been a challenge. I hope he stays for you too, my brother. You deserve happiness. Does Patrick seem happy with you?"

"He did before Tavik's comments. We have been intimate with each other, too. But you're right, he is difficult to read. I'm not sure yet if he truly wants to stay or if he is only trying to show his thanks to the clan by helping where he can."

The conversation slowed when a sorvik came closer. Rath jerked his chin in that direction, urging me to take it. Carefully, I slid out of the watching tree, keeping against it to hide myself. The sorvik had yet to notice me. I pulled my bow from my back, setting an arrow against it.

"Take your time," Rath murmured so low, I almost didn't hear it. "Remember to breathe."

It had been a long time since I learned to hunt. I knew to do these things. But instead of being indignant of his lessons, I listened to my friend, waiting and taking slow breaths until the sorvik was in a good position. I let my arrow loose, pulling out a second immediately in case I missed. I didn't. My arrow lodged in the sorvik's chest, and it dropped to the ground with a whine.

Rath dropped from the tree, grinning as he gripped my shoulder. "Excellent shot, brother."

I made a face at him. "It is not my first sorvik. You know this."

"I do," he nodded. "But you have been distracted as of late. It has affected your skill. I only wish to commend you when you put aside your troubles and bring great honor to our clan."

I settled a little at his words. I *had* been distracted. My jealousy of him split my focus. Then Patrick arrived, and I wanted so much to return to him that I didn't give my whole self to the hunt. I was an excellent hunter if I focused on the task. I needed only to slow down and remember that.

Rath helped me bring the sorvik to the waiting tree. He had more hunting to do, and I had herbs to look for to bring to Yamileth. Before we separated, he put his hand on my shoulder and spoke low to me. "Whatever you choose to do about Tavik, you have my support. And my sword, should you need it."

"Let's hope it doesn't come to that," I grumbled. I was angry with Tavik, but I had yet to reach the urge to kill him. If he kept insulting Patrick, though, the choice would be taken from me. I would claim Patrick, should he choose me back. And I would never let him come to harm. Not even from my own clan brothers.

My leg was throbbing after making the morning meal, so Yamileth sent me to Verus's tent to rest. She said I could return to help with the afternoon meal only if I rested, so I didn't argue with her. She had yet to tell me what she planned on doing about Tavik and his friend, but I did my best not to think about it. It was out of my hands, and I just wanted to forget the words that were said.

I was lying down, but not asleep, when Verus showed up. He looked incensed, and I wasn't sure why. I thought maybe he was angry with me until he climbed on top of me and captured my lips. I gasped in surprise, and he took full advantage, sliding his tongue into my mouth. A rush of arousal swamped me, and I was helpless to do anything about it. Verus's mouth dominated mine, and I could only hang on and let him have his way with me.

I was so distracted by his mouth, I didn't notice his hands until they were tugging on my tunic. When he broke the kiss long enough to pull it over my head, I breathlessly asked, "What—"

Verus didn't let me get the entire question out before taking my mouth again. He sucked on my tongue, and I moaned against his lips, my fingers digging into his tunic to keep him close.

Unlike last time, Verus seemed to be in a hurry. I wasn't sure why, and I didn't have time to ask. He carefully stripped off my trousers and smallclothes, leaving me bare beneath him, then set to work kissing every inch of me, until I was breathless and my whole body felt flushed.

Lost in the sweet way he touched me, I didn't expect him to take me into his mouth. I choked on a gasp, arching my back, as he sucked me down to the root. I'd never felt anything like it before. Hot wet heat wrapped around my member, his tongue flattening along the vein underneath. I fisted the blankets beneath me, my head thrown back as I tried to get any words past my throat. If he didn't slow down, I was going to finish in his mouth.

I opened my mouth to beg him, but for what? For more? To slow down? I wasn't sure. All that came out was a whimper either way.

Verus released me with a pop, lifting his head to lock eyes with me.

"The sounds you make drive me to distraction. I want to taste every inch of you, ravsol. Will you let me?"

I still couldn't get any words out. My cock throbbed in his grip, and I felt certain I would explode if he put his mouth on me again, but still I nodded. He lit up like I'd given him a gift, smiling at me, before he dipped his head again, skipping past my length to draw one of my balls into his mouth. I groaned in surprise, feeling them draw up tightly. I was so close, my stomach quivered with it. But I didn't expect what he'd do next.

He moved my good leg up and out, spreading me wider. It might have embarrassed me had I had the capacity to feel anything other than aroused. I felt his fingers grip my ass, felt his mouth move lower, but I didn't expect his tongue to slide over my hole. Pleasure sparked through me in ways I didn't think possible, and I felt my arousal climb higher than it ever had before. I wanted more, wanted to beg for it, but I could only moan and gasp until he pushed his tongue inside me and I fell apart at the seams. My release coursed through me like a lightning storm, and I couldn't draw in a breath until it passed. When I finally went boneless, I realized I'd squeezed my eyes shut and pried them open, looking at Verus with wonder.

"What... was... that...?" I asked between heavy breaths.

His grin was wicked when he said, "I told you I wanted to taste you everywhere. Did you like it?"

I could only nod rapidly. That was amazing. There were no words to describe it. And when Verus dipped to kiss me and I could taste myself on his lips, my cock twitched with one final aftershock of pleasure.

While it still made me nervous, it felt wrong not to offer to give him pleasure in return. When Verus pulled away, leaning his forehead against mine, I felt my voice shake as I asked him, "Can I do the same to you?"

He raised his eyebrows slowly. "You want to eat my ass?"

That... hadn't been what I meant, but now I was a little curious. And I didn't think it would hurt like the other thing might. I bit my lip, studying him. "Would you like it?"

A light dusting of pink overtook his cheeks, stunning me. He looked embarrassed to admit it, which was absolutely adorable.

"I do like it, but I wouldn't ask you to do more than you're comfortable with. You are still new, and I don't want to rush you."

My heart swelled a little, and I smiled shyly at him. "I'd like to try…"

He'd mentioned the noises I made earlier. I was too distracted by what he was doing to truly listen, but I wanted to see if I could bring noises from him as well. Verus sucked in a shaky breath like he was nervous, but the eagerness in his expression made me laugh. He took off his clothes, and I watched with greedy eyes as every beautiful inch of skin was exposed.

When he was bare, he looked down at me with heat and excitement in his eyes that made my stomach quicken and my cock twitch, despite the explosive finish just minutes before. A wicked grin flashed across his face again, and this time, when he climbed on top of me, straddling my chest and then leaning over to brace his arms on either side of my legs, he was facing the other way.

I honestly wasn't expecting this part of him to be sexy, but it was. Getting to see the most intimate part of him, to touch him like he touched me. It took my breath away. I couldn't help but run my hands over him, up his thighs and over his ass, touching every inch of him. When my thumb brushed over his hole, it contracted, and he groaned in response. I did it again, my stomach jumping when he rocked a little in a silent plea for more.

I wanted to give it to him. More than anything, I wanted to give him what he needed. With my hands on his hips, I pulled him backward and, ignoring the nerves fluttering in my belly, flicked my tongue over his hole.

Fourteen

When I thought of one day finding a tribute of my own, I never expected this. In our clan, we were raised with the idea of caring for our tributes. I thought only to bring Patrick pleasure. I would have been happy to only do this to him forever. But when he asked so sweetly, I couldn't resist.

He was timid at first, using little flicks of his tongue that drove me insane with want. I kept that to myself, only letting the sounds of pleasure escape my lips. The more sounds I made, the more confident he grew, until he was licking my entrance like it was his favorite treat. I writhed under his ministrations, gasping and moaning, trying hard to keep myself away from his injured leg. When his tongue breached me, my mouth fell open and a louder groan escaped me as I rocked back for more.

My cock throbbed and jerked with the need for release. I wanted to beg him to use his fingers, to do more, but Patrick was still new to sex. I wanted to show him first before asking him to do more. Instead, I shifted my weight to one arm, using the other to stroke myself. It wouldn't take long for me to come. His tongue was magic.

I heard and felt him moan, the vibrations against my hole making my eyes roll back. When I looked down, I saw his cock swell, and the thought of him enjoying this with me set me off. I came with a shout, covering his chest and stomach with my release. I stroked myself through it, shivering when he gave me one final long lick.

Careful not to hurt him, I climbed off and rolled onto my side. I was too far away from him, my head near his cock, but my body shook from the force of my climax, and I needed a moment before I returned to him.

"Verus..." His voice was a little tight, like he was nervous about something. Summoning enough energy, I shifted to my elbow so I could better see him.

"What is it?"

His freckled skin was pink, and he sunk his teeth into his bottom lip, worrying it nervously. I sat up fully, tugging lightly on his chin to release the trapped flesh.

"What bothers you, my ravsol?"

My stomach sank for a moment. Did I push him too far? Was it too much? Did he only do it for me? Was it—

"Do you... Do you like to be taken? Or do you like taking?"

The question confused me, and I frowned at him for a moment. His blush deepened and he gestured to me, or more specifically to my cock. Realization sank in and I sucked in a breath.

"Oh! I like both. Does this... bother you?"

There were some men in the clan who believed the one who took was stronger than the one taken. I didn't believe that. It felt good both ways. Why would it make me weak just because I wanted both?

He shook his head quickly, nibbling on his lip again. "I've never done either... I'm curious..."

Relief and joy settled in my chest, and I shifted myself so that I was lying beside him, my face inches from his. Cupping his cheek, I kissed him softly. "We will try everything you wish to, ravsol. I'm happy to explore your preferences with you."

His blush went down his neck and onto his chest, but he looked happy, and he kissed me back passionately when I reached for him again. I would need to talk to Orthorr soon about my intentions with Patrick. I wanted him as my bondmate. I just hoped my clan could accept that. I wasn't sure if it had ever been done, to claim a bondmate who was not part of the clan or our life, as a brother or tribute. Patrick would be the first.

I kept Patrick with me for the rest of the day, mostly because he looked like he was in pain when he tried to go back to Yamileth to help. I'd needed her help to get him to rest, but he eventually agreed and I spent the rest of the night pampering him like he deserved.

Patrick woke up with me like he had each morning since he joined me in my tent and I smothered him in kisses until he was laughing. I brought him to the cooking tent after we washed up at the river. I saw his grimace of discomfort when he sat down—he was obviously in pain—but he liked working and wanted to give back to the clan as much as he could. Worried about him, I stuck close, sitting on the ground by his stool with a basket full of herbs Yamileth demanded I bundle for her so they could dry.

"If you're going to be in here, make yourself useful," she grouched, hobbling away to check on something else. Her tent always smelled so delicious, and I was glad no one heard my stomach grumbling. I'd worked up an appetite with Patrick the day prior.

While wrapping some twine around the bundles, I watched Patrick work. He had strong muscles in his arms from working the dough every day, and a serene smile on his face. He was happy working with Yamileth. I hoped that was a good thing.

"Have you cooked a meal yet?" I asked, because while I wanted to let him focus, I was also desperate for his attention.

He shook his head, smiling warmly at me. "Not yet. I asked Yamileth to give me the tasks first. I wanted to show her I know what I'm doing."

I shot a questioning look at Yamileth, who nodded. "He is knowledgeable in cooking, but I need to see his skill before I allow him to cook for the clan." She narrowed her eyes on Patrick. "When your tasks are done, cook me something small so I can see what you can do."

I jerked to face Patrick, giving him my biggest pout. He snickered at me.

"Alright. I'll make enough for both of you. Don't make that face."

"Why? Does it do something to you?" I asked, waggling my eyebrows. He laughed harder, which had been my goal, and I beamed in triumph. I wanted so much to make him happy.

"You two are sickeningly sweet," Yamileth commented, making Patrick blush hotly. He didn't look upset about the comment, though, a small pleased smile pulling at his lips. He was happy, and I would do anything to keep him that way.

I helped Patrick and Yamileth until Rath came to find me and dragged me away to hunt. He looked about as happy as I felt to leave, and when I raised an eyebrow at him, he made a face.

"You try waking up with an amorous bondmate and feeling excitement for doing anything but staying in bed with him," he grumbled.

I nodded in commiseration. "I understand. I had no wish to leave the warmth of our bed this morning either. Had Patrick not had his own work to do, I would have tried to convince him to stay."

As we guided our stallions through the trees, Rath asked, "Is he well enough to help? He is still in pain, is he not?"

"He is," I agreed with a sigh. "But he's determined to help."

Rath hummed, keeping his voice low so as not to scare the game away. "Then support him and do what you can to ease his pain when he is resting. Perhaps more furs for sleeping, to make him more comfortable."

That was a good thought. Patrick hadn't complained about sleeping with me, but he was also not one to complain. He had yet to say much about his pain, even though I could tell he was uncomfortable. More furs would be good. I would also speak with Zoya and ask her what ways I could help Patrick. She said she would monitor him, but surely there was more I could do.

After catching a few larger fowl, I spent some time gathering the herbs Yamileth needed that were farther in the forest. There were others in the clan who would gather herbs for her, but none would venture this far without an escort. It was faster for me to do it.

I was tucking the last of the herbs away in my pouch when I heard a familiar voice behind me.

"You should have told me you were lonely. I would have taken care of you," Tavik purred.

Spinning around, I scowled at him. "What are you doing out here?"

Tavik was not a hunter. He was a warrior, and not a very good one. He was not taught how to defend against the more dangerous creatures of the forest, the ones who were not easily defeated by steel alone. He didn't belong out here without an escort.

"I wanted to speak with you," he said, the suggestive purr still in his throat. "Surely you aren't getting your needs cared for by that casak."

I bared my teeth at the use of the foul term. "Watch it," I warned.

He strode closer, all cocky confidence. It was that attitude that made me uninterested. He had propositioned me before. I had no desire to waste my time with men like him.

"You know I am more a man than he will ever be. Let me prove it to you."

He reached for my trousers, like he believed I would let him touch me willingly. I was quick to block him, drawing out my sword and putting it against his throat.

"Do not touch me."

The air of seduction on his face faded, and he glared at me. "Why do you deny me? You always have. I am better than everyone in our clan and still you push me away."

I scoffed, rolling my eyes at him. "It is that attitude that puts me off your advances. You are full of yourself and only interested in your own wants. It would be no different if I did indulge you. Go slake your lust with someone else. I am not interested."

From the look in his eyes, he wanted to push the issue, but with my blade at his neck, he had no choice but to step back. He glowered at me, lifting his chin stubbornly.

"I am better than he is. I will prove it to you. And when you realize you are wrong, you will come crawling."

Snorting, I gave him a bland look. "Only in your wildest fantasies, Tavik. Go back to the village. You do not belong out here."

With a final glare, he left, stomping off toward the village. I had no choice but to follow him, as it would dishonor me to let him come to harm while he was alone with me. I walked him as far as the gathering tree, where a few others waited. I jerked my chin at Rhos.

"Take him home. He is foolish to be out here."

That got me an incredulous look from Tavik, but Rhos only nodded, nudging Tavik on his way when he stayed rooted in place, silently seething.

Once they disappeared through the trees, Rhos's blood brother Orvak raised an eyebrow at me.

"I heard tell that you were wrapped around the one found in the forest. Did you really stoop so low as to give in to Tavik?"

My face screwed up in disgust. "Never. He sought me out to plead for it. I told him no. I only want Patrick."

Fifteen

After helping with the clan meal prep, I finally took the time to create a meal for Yamileth and Verus. She'd requested it a few days prior, but with the pain I was in once my usual tasks were done, she decided to put it off until I could move better on my own. I wasn't happy about it, but I couldn't argue with her. So I waited until I felt like she was distracted enough that I could get away with it without her noticing my pain.

I decided on a meal that could easily be made in large quantities, scaling the recipe down for a smaller batch. I didn't rush it, and took the time while it was cooking to help Yamileth with the normal cooking. I finished just after the noise of the clan meal had died down, and Verus had returned from his hunt.

Scooping two servings into bowls, I handed them to Yamileth and Verus, shifting uneasily on my stool as I waited for them to taste it. If I had been able to stand, I would have been bouncing on my toes. I felt a little better when Verus's eyes lit up, and he began to shovel large mouthfuls into his mouth, but I held my breath as I waited for Yamileth's opinion. She was the one who would decide if it was good enough for me to cook beside her.

She hummed, setting the bowl down on the table beside her. My heart sank, worried she didn't like it, and when she stood, I braced myself for the worst. My eyes were squeezed shut, and I didn't see her coming until she pulled me into a hug. Startled, I could only cling to her.

"I waited a long time for someone to be good enough to work beside me. I am glad the fates brought you here. Perhaps now I will finally have a chance to rest."

"You like it?" I croaked, looking up at her. Tears burned my eyes, and a lump formed in my throat. I had been so worried about her reaction, it was hard to comprehend what she was saying.

"It is delicious. I look forward to seeing what else you can create. I only stopped eating it because you looked like you would pass out from holding your breath," she teased.

Relief flooded me, and I let out a watery laugh, hugging her a little tighter. If she liked my cooking and wanted me to work beside her, it would hopefully be a point in my favor when I eventually asked to stay. As long as that was what Verus wanted.

"She is not wrong, Patrick," Verus said cheerfully. "Is there more? I think one bowl is not enough."

When Yamileth finally released me and I looked over at him, Verus's bowl was already empty, and his eyes were locked on the pot the rest of the stew rested in. I felt a smile tug at my lips as I put my hand out for his bowl, scooping him another large helping. He immediately tucked in to enjoy it, making happy humming noises as he inhaled his meal. His obvious pleasure made me blush, and I was suddenly glad I'd made extra. If my food made him happy, then I never wanted to stop cooking for him.

A rustle drew my focus to the entrance of the tent, where a familiar barbarian stepped inside. Finn's bondmate was an intimidating man, big and bulky like Tavik, but with a softness in his eyes that Tavik didn't have. He guided Finn in with a hand on his lower back, his expression patient as he urged the shy man inside.

Yamileth frowned at the visitors, her eyes narrowed. "What do you need?"

Rath shook his head, a patient smile on his face. "Nothing. Finn wanted to spend more time with Patrick. He is here to ask to join him while I train Evak to hunt."

Happiness bubbled in my chest, and I shifted my gaze to Finn, who was blushing fiercely. We'd only really spent time together to learn, never just to hang out. He was the reason I was so comfortable with the language already. I would be happy to spend more time with him.

"Join us, brother," Verus called, motioning Finn closer. "You need to try Patrick's food. It is delicious."

Curiosity overrode his shyness, and Finn came closer, accepting the bowl Verus handed him after he scooped Finn out a portion. It was a little embarrassing having him praise me like that—my food wasn't that big of a deal—but I chose not to say anything. It was nice to hear, and I didn't want to discourage him.

Taking an empty stool, Finn took a small bite of the food. He looked surprised, and a bright smile overtook his face when he looked up at me. "Is this butcher's stew?"

I nodded once. "It's a recipe I'm familiar with, and it can be made for a large number of people. I thought it was a good idea to show my skill."

He offered a bite to his bondmate, who hadn't yet left, waiting to make sure Finn was comfortable and happy. Rath was harder to read than Finn was, his expression more contemplative, but Finn was practically bouncing in his seat with excitement.

"It's really good! What else can you make? I love the food here, but there are a few things I miss from home. I never learned to cook, though, so I've never had any hope of recreating them."

Tipping my head side to side, I answered, "I'm more comfortable with baking than cooking, but I know a few recipes off the top of my head. And I've always been a quick study when it comes to cooking. What kinds of things do you miss?"

Rath and Verus left while we talked about recipes and favorite foods, and how I could recreate them out here. Not all the food was the same, since the barbarians foraged instead of farming like the towns, but I didn't think it would be too hard to change up the recipe just a little to get the same results. Yamileth threw in her suggestions for substitutions as well, and mentioned a few recipes she planned on teaching me so that the knowledge would be passed down.

It was nice to spend time just chatting about the things I enjoyed. It made me feel like I belonged here. And the hope that I could stay only grew the longer I spent with these people. Gods, I hoped I could stay.

I WAS GETTING READY FOR SLEEP THAT NIGHT WHEN VERUS DUCKED INTO the tent, his arms full with a bundle of furs. I tipped my head, studying him with a frown.

"Are you cold?"

He huffed out a laugh, dropping the bundle onto the bed without care. "No. But you are uncomfortable while sleeping. I am making our bed softer for you."

Warmth and happiness spread through my chest, making me feel a little giddy. Verus never hid how much he cared. He went above and beyond to make sure I was comfortable and happy. I couldn't have been more grateful that it was him who found me in the forest.

Desperate to show him how much it meant to me, as soon as he got close, I fisted his tunic, dragging him down so I could pepper his face with kisses. He chuckled, wrapping me in his arms and kissing me back soundly. I hadn't intended it to lead anywhere, I only wanted to thank him, but his tongue licked along the seam of my lips, and when I opened up for him, he groaned into it. He pulled away too quickly, and I whimpered at the loss.

Pressing his forehead against mine, Verus whispered, "Zoya is to come and check on your healing. I do not wish to greet her while aroused. She would never let me live it down."

My cheeks flushed bright red at the thought. No, I really didn't want anyone to walk in while we were intimate. I was still getting used to the idea of Verus being affectionate with me while around the clan. I didn't want to embarrass myself any further by getting too caught up in his kisses.

Smacking a kiss on my lips, Verus scooped me up and moved me to sit by the table in the corner while he untied the furs and started fussing with them. I was watching him with a sappy smile when a feminine voice called out.

"Can I come in?"

Verus's head popped up, and he answered, "Come in," while smiling brightly. Zoya swept into the tent, her rounded belly leading the way.

"Good evening," she greeted, moving to sit beside me. "How are you, Patrick?"

I lifted my shoulder, wrinkling my nose a little. "The splint is a little uncomfortable. Especially while trying to sleep."

Zoya nodded in understanding, her gaze straying to where Verus was still fussing with the furs. A smile tugged at her lips. "I can see your protector is working to make that a little easier. I understand that it's uncomfortable, but it's for the best. It's only been a few weeks since you were hurt. Do you mind if I take a look?"

She looked over the injury, humming and murmuring to herself. "It looks like it's healing well. The swelling has gone down and it looks like everything is as it should be. Are you just uncomfortable or does the pain keep you awake?"

I shook my head. "It's not terrible. Only when I'm moving around a lot does it hurt. Yamileth has me sitting on a stool while I help her, so I can rest as much as possible."

"Oh, you're helping Yami?" she asked curiously.

"Patrick is a wonderful cook," Verus interjected. "He has many plans for meals he will cook for the clan. I am looking forward to it."

I felt my cheeks flush from his praise. Even when my business became more popular in town, I didn't receive as much praise as Verus showered me with. I hoped he wasn't just saying it because we were intimate together. His words meant a lot, and I would be devastated if they turned out to be false.

"I'm looking forward to trying it," Zoya said, giving me a soft smile. "You look like you're healing well to me. Continue to rest often, and don't push yourself too hard helping Yami. She'll understand if you need to take a break."

"Is there anything else we can do to encourage healing?" Verus asked, coming to squat beside me. He ran his fingers through my hair, his expression clouded with worry. "I do not like it when he is in pain."

"These things take time, Verus," she scolded, though the warmth in her eyes said she wasn't annoyed with him for pushing. "But I'll make a poultice that will encourage healing if it will make you feel better. We'll need to make sure nothing touches it until it dries, so you won't be able to get dressed right away, but it should get you back on your feet soon enough."

I both looked forward to getting back on my feet and dreaded it at the same time. As long as I was injured, I wasn't required to leave. I could just stay here and be with Verus. And there was no place in the world I would rather be.

Sixteen

Clearing my throat, I waited anxiously for Orthorr to permit me entrance to his tent. I had been working up the nerve to have this conversation with him, and I worried about the outcome. Patrick was going to get better soon. Zoya put on the poultice this morning and said it would likely only be a few more weeks before Patrick was on his feet again. I needed to make sure he was allowed to stay once he was well again.

"Enter," Orthorr called out.

Following his instruction, I ducked my head into his tent, not surprised to find two others with him. Uttin was likely next in line to become clan leader, as he had the mind for leadership. He was in charge of picking up the tributes from the towns. He met with others like him from nearby clans to distribute them, and the rest were brought here until they were ready to look for their bondmates. It was unknown to me why our clan was the first stopping point for the tributes, but I never thought much about it. It was just the way things were.

Beside him sat one of the elders, Morak, who made the leathers. I was curious why he was there but knew better than to ask. Morak didn't appreciate nosy clan members.

"Verus," Orthorr greeted with a dip of his chin. Putting my fist across my chest, I bowed slightly in greeting.

"Clan leader. There is something I wish to discuss with you, if you have the time."

Orthorr gestured for me to join them at the small round table, and I sat in Morak's place when he got up to leave.

"I will make my request to Rath, then, Clan Leader," he said over his shoulder.

"Do so," Orthorr encouraged. "If he has concerns, tell him to speak with me."

Curiosity bubbled in my chest, and I couldn't help but ask, "What do you need from Rath?"

As the best hunter, Rath was in charge of the hunts and those who hunted for the clan. If Morak intended to make a request to Rath, I would hear of it eventually.

Like I expected, Morak didn't reply outside of an irritated look cast in my direction. He walked out without a word to me. Uttin sighed.

"He acts as though it is a great secret that he needs more hides. The hunters will need to focus on larger game for a time to get him what he needs."

I nodded slowly. Usually, we mixed our catches so there was a plethora of meats and furs or feathers, so that everyone in the clan could get what they needed. However, if there was a need for something more specific, for a time we could focus on that. It would mean hunting outside the forest, though. The coiwaks that provided the hides that Morak preferred traveled in herds outside the forest. It took longer to get those hides, as the herd would run once a single coiwak was taken down, and it was dangerous to be near the herd on the run. We would need to begin the process of hunting them all over again to get enough for Morak to be happy.

I wasn't looking forward to that hunt. It would take a week at the very least. That meant I would be away from Patrick for a time, which made my heart ache. I had no wish to be apart from him.

"Verus? What is the reason you came to see me?" Orthorr asked, pulling my focus back to him. I blinked rapidly for a moment, almost forgetting my intentions in meeting with him, before I remembered my goals.

"I wish to bond with Patrick," I told him, my heart beginning to gallop in my chest. "I do not wish for him to leave once he is healed."

Orthorr frowned, his lips pursed. "Such a bonding has not been done before. Outsiders are not invited into our clans unless they are tributes."

Uttin tipped his head, his expression thoughtful. "Does Patrick wish to stay?"

I hesitated. I had yet to truly ask him. I worried about his answer more than Orthorr's. "He seems happy here. He is working with Yamileth now with the cooking, and he feels safe with me. I did not wish to rush him in deciding by telling him my intentions. Nor did I want to get his hopes up if it is not possible," I hedged.

Orthorr nodded in understanding. "It is good not to push while he is healing. Let me think on it for a time. There may need to be a discussion with other clan leaders. Like when we accepted Finn as a tribute, it could lead to a precedent by accepting an outsider to join us."

That made no sense to me. Such things were beyond my understanding. I shot a questioning look at Uttin, who was kind enough to explain.

"We believe by accepting Finn as tribute, it will mean more male tributes in the future. As there are males in other clans who wish for a male to bond with, we have accepted this possibility. Letting Patrick join us without cause will be much the same. It could lead to more townsfolk in the future showing up on our lands requesting to join us." His brows drew tighter together. "I doubt it would happen often, though. The townsfolk still fear us."

"But if they are in a situation like Patrick?" I pushed. "He fled for his safety. Would we really turn people away?"

Orthorr shook his head. "Never. It would go against the gods to do such a cruel thing. But there is a difference between providing refuge until someone is ready to move on and accepting them into our clan. He does not know our ways, and if a steady stream of outsiders join us, it could risk our way of life. It needs to be considered carefully. I'm not saying no, Verus. Give me time to think on it. Meanwhile, you should speak with

Patrick. If he does not even wish to stay, then the question could be pointless."

That was true. While I felt that Patrick enjoyed being with me, I didn't know his plans for the future. I was a little afraid to ask. I would go with him, should he choose to leave, but I didn't want to. My clan was my family, my home. I wanted him to stay here with me.

I WAS WAYLAID BY RATH BEFORE I COULD SEEK PATRICK OUT AFTER MY meeting with Orthorr. He gathered the other hunters, relaying the same information Uttin shared with me earlier.

"Two will stay behind to do the daily hunts for the clan. The rest will join me to seek out the herd."

Torn between wanting to stay so I could be with Patrick and wanting to go to support my brother, I stayed silent as Rath spoke on what to pack and where the herd was last seen. I had always participated in the longer hunts. I enjoyed them. The hunt itself was a challenge, since the coiwak were easily spooked and would run a great distance to get themselves to safety before they could be approached again. Rath hoped with enough people, we could take out all the coiwak needed at once instead of playing chase, which would make the hunt extra challenging. I also loved the camaraderie. Spending time with my fellow hunters was always fun, and I felt more connected to my clan after a long hunt.

But Patrick…

I worried about leaving him. Zoya said it would be a few more weeks before Patrick was healed enough to even walk again, but what if he healed faster than expected? What if by the time I got back, he was already gone? I'd told Orthorr my intentions, and I had hopes that he wouldn't make Patrick leave before I returned, but hope would only get me so far.

"Verus."

Rath's voice caught my attention, and I looked up to find the rest of the hunters already gone and Rath watching me with a frown. I told myself to not be so distant with him about my problems, so instead of pretending I was fine, I told him of my worries.

"What if Patrick is gone before I can return?"

Rath frowned deeply. "He is not healed yet."

"No, but Zoya said a few more weeks. These hunts take time. I worry that he will be gone before I can return."

My clan brother's expression turned into a grimace. "I have no intention of dragging this out. I do not wish to be away from Finn for that long. I would ask that you come with me, my brother. We are a good team. I believe we can finish things quickly with you by my side. But I'll understand if you wish to stay with Patrick. I will assign you to stay and hunt for the clan meals instead."

I'd honestly not thought about how Rath would take this journey. His bonding with Finn was still new. They had yet to be separated from each other beyond hunts for meals. Rath had even more reason to stay behind, but he would go anyway to serve our clan. I did not wish to drag out his suffering by sending him off without me.

"I will go with you."

Rath shook his head. "You do not—"

"You are my brother," I interrupted, my voice firm. "Besides, you're right. You cannot do it without me. I'm just that good."

He snorted and rolled his eyes, shoving me away from him. I snickered and shoved him back, starting a game of wrestling between us. It always ended up with him winning—he was a cheat— but it reminded me of our friendship. I would be by his side because he asked me to be. And I could only hope that Patrick would still be here when I returned.

Rath had me in a headlock when Finn and Patrick joined us. Both looked amused at our antics. I did not wish to lose in front of Patrick, so I fought harder to get free, but my victory was short lived. Rath released me to go to his bondmate. I did not actually escape on my own.

Balanced on his crutches, Patrick smiled at me. "You are brave to face him."

Carefully, I gathered him in my arms so he could rest. "He is a cheat. He only won because of this."

Rath's head whipped around, and he glared at me. "I am no cheat. You are just jealous."

I lifted my chin in challenge, but with Patrick in my arms and Finn wrapped around Rath's waist, neither of us was willing to have another match. We would need to truly test our strength another time. Perhaps on the hunt.

The reminder made me sigh. I needed to tell Patrick. I hoped he wouldn't be too angry with me for leaving.

Seventeen

My favorite place in the world was in Verus's arms. Even after weeks of being with the clan, it still surprised me that he could carry me around so easily. He didn't even look strained while doing it. His broad smile never wavered as he carried me back to his tent. It was no wonder they had to hunt daily. I'd seen the amount of meat the clan needed to have members so thickly muscled fed and taken care of. It was astounding.

Once I was settled on the thick furs, Verus claimed my lips in a hot kiss. I never had to ask for affection from him. He gave it freely, sought it out the minute we were close to one another. It made me feel loved and wanted every single time. That someone as perfect as him would want me as badly as Verus seemed to felt like a dream come true.

I ran my hands up his thighs after he straddled my hips, still thrilled I could touch him freely without worrying about someone finding us. It was finally starting to sink in that I could be with him without restriction here, without needing to hide. Not even in the towns where same sex relationships were legal were people so obvious about it. I'd never heard of a town where two men could walk down the street hand in hand, much less one man carrying another around in a bridal carry or kissing him before he left for work. They kept that part of their life private.

Here, I could just be with Verus without consequences. It felt a little like heaven.

Verus hummed, leaning into my touch as my palms slid up his chest. I wanted to touch every inch of him all the time. He had the kind of body that needed to be worshiped.

"Patrick," he groaned, grinding his butt against my erection. I moaned into his mouth, gripping his hips to encourage him to do it again.

Rocking his hips, Verus teased me with the promise of more. We hadn't gone a day since the first time he brought me to completion without getting off together, but we hadn't done this before. I wanted to, and I wanted him to take me too, but Verus was taking it slow. He was worried about hurting me.

Still, I couldn't help but encourage him, slipping my hands to grip his cheeks and knead them. His groan was filled with lust, and he ground a little faster against me, like his control was slipping and he couldn't help himself. Each roll of his hips made me gasp, and I felt myself edging closer and closer to release.

Ripping his mouth away from mine, Verus moaned. "Patrick, I need—" He gasped and shuddered when I slipped my hands into his trousers and squeezed again. "Oh gods, I need it."

"Please!" I wasn't above begging at this point. I knew what he wanted, and I was desperate to give it to him.

Like my *please* was the permission he was waiting for, Verus jerked away from me, yanking off his boots and trousers and tossing them aside. He went after my clothes with the same urgency, and I barely had time to draw in a breath before I was naked underneath him. I had no time to feel embarrassed about it, my focus glued to the beautiful man above me. He snatched the oil out of the chest nearby and dribbled some on his fingers. Despite my lack of experience, I knew why he needed it and reached for it, wishing I could help prepare him.

Verus pushed my hands away, shaking his head. "If you do it, I'll come. I need you too much, ravsol. Let me just—" He shuddered, and while I couldn't see it, watching his face as he stretched himself almost pushed me into completion.

Wrapping my hand around his cock was both a distraction and a small punishment for denying me. He shouted in surprise, thrusting into my hand and back onto his fingers. I watched, fascinated, as he fought to keep his orgasm at bay, his teeth gritted together and his eyes squeezed shut.

He shook his head, prying open his eyes to look at me. "I can't—I can't take anymore. I need you too much."

Happiness and desire swirled in my chest, making me just as needy as he was. "I need you too. Please, Verus."

He groaned in response, pulling his fingers free and spreading the excess oil over my length. I had to squeeze my eyes shut to stop myself from coming just from his touch, so I wasn't prepared when he notched the head of my cock against his entrance and sank down onto me.

My eyes flew open on a gasp, and I scrambled for purchase, the pleasure out of this world. Tight, slick heat wrapped around my member, and it took every ounce of control I had not to come instantly.

"V-Verus!"

"Gods, you feel so good," he groaned, rocking his hips to take more of me. His head was thrown back, his eyes shut. The image only made the experience hotter, and I whimpered, fighting back the urge to come.

He paused after taking all of me, both of us panting. I was grateful for the reprieve, giving me time to pull myself together. I wanted it to be good for him, too. I wanted to make him feel as good as he made me feel.

"Are you okay?" he asked, his fingers drifting over my cheek.

I hummed, lifting my chin in a silent request for a kiss. He gave it without question, smothering me with kisses. Not full of passion but what felt like love instead. They were sweet and caring and made tears well in my eyes. If Verus loved me, I think I would die happy. It would be like a dream come true.

Verus shifted, and I could feel the mood change as he grew restless. Running my hands down his back, I gripped his thighs, encouraging him to move. His answering moan was like music to my ears. He started rocking his hips like he had before, only this time with me inside him. My fingers flexed and my toes curled as pleasure coiled in my belly with every move.

It wasn't just the pleasure of being inside him that set me aflame. The noises he made, the ecstasy on his face, it all added to the moment. I couldn't look away.

"You're beautiful," I murmured.

~

Patrick's whispered comment made me melt. I didn't think the moment could get any better, but with each caress along my skin, each murmur of encouragement, I was proven wrong.

His hand wrapped around the back of my neck, drawing me back down for another passionate kiss. Our tongues tangled, a mimicry of what was happening below. With every grind of my hips, the heat in my belly expanded, ready to explode in an instant. I craved it, craved the release he offered me. Craved the feeling of being claimed by him.

Shifting movement caught my attention as Patrick's good leg drew up, giving him a little more leverage. He snapped his hips, meeting mine on my next downward thrust, and I cried out in surprise from the force of it. I wanted to protest that he would hurt himself, but I couldn't form words. Patrick's thrusts only added to the pleasure, until I couldn't see straight.

"Patrick! Patrick!" I chanted, slamming my hips down to take him again. Each time his hips met mine, it felt like lightning, heat and pleasure coursing through my body. I wasn't sure how much more I could take, but I wanted it to last forever. I never wanted this moment to end.

My head flew back as Patrick fisted my cock, stroking it in time with his thrusts. The pairing was too much, and I came with a shout, grinding down on Patrick's cock to feel him deep inside me. It set him off, and he writhed beneath me, the heat of his release filling my channel. Claiming me.

I collapsed on top of him, my body throbbing with aftershocks of pleasure. I was careful to keep my weight off his leg, but I was too wiped out to move fully away. And the thought of losing the connection between us felt like torment.

Patrick's arms slid around my shoulders, hugging me tightly against him. I let out a sigh of happiness as I hugged him back. This was the perfect place to be. I wished I could stay here forever, with us wrapped around each other.

The reminder that I couldn't made me sigh, and I buried my face against his neck to hide from the truth.

Strong fingers cupped the back of my head, stroking my hair gently. "Verus? What's wrong?"

He knew me so well already that he could feel the shift in my mood. Despite not wishing to, I pulled away to look at him, pouting when his softened cock slipped from inside me. Had it been possible, I would've wished him to stay that way all night.

Patrick's hand cupped my face, his thumb stroking over my cheek as he studied me with a worried expression. "Did I hurt you?"

A smile tugged at my lips, and I turned to press a kiss to the middle of his palm. "No, ravsol. I felt no pain. I am wishing I didn't have to leave you."

His brow furrowed, and true fear swept over his face. I realized my mistake immediately and was quick to reassure him.

"Not forever, my Patrick. We must go on a long hunt. The coiwak move too frequently for us to return home each night. We must track them and that takes time. Time I must spend away from you. It hurts my heart to think about, but I must go for my clan."

The fear settled, and sadness and understanding took its place. "Okay... How long will you be gone?"

With a heavy sigh, I rolled to my side to remove my weight from him. I stuck close, pressing myself against his side, and tucked my arm under my head to pillow it. "At least a week. Perhaps more. It depends on where the herd is and if they notice our approach. They are not dangerous creatures, but they are fast. It is hard to take more than one at a time, and they run after each is taken down, forcing us to chase them. It will not be an easy hunt."

"When do you go?"

I didn't want to answer. It would only hurt him. We had such little time before I had to leave.

He seemed to understand without me saying the words aloud. "So soon?"

Leaning to rest my forehead against his, I gave him a soft kiss. "I'm sorry. Morak needs hides tanned before we move on from this place. We must go quickly to have them finished in time."

"What for?" he asked curiously.

I hummed, thinking about it. "Many things. Boots, straps to tie up the tents, bags, armor. His leathers are needed for repairs as we move. His work is very important for our clan so we try to give him what he needs when he needs it." Pressing a kiss to his temple, I hugged him a little tighter. "Promise you'll wait for me, ravsol. I cannot bring myself to go if you won't be here when I get back."

His fingers dug into my skin as he clung to me. "I promise. As long as you promise to come back."

"Always, ravsol. I will always come back to you."

Eighteen

I woke up early the next morning, carefully pulling out of Verus's arms. He said the hunt would be long, which meant for the most part, they would probably be feeding themselves as they tracked the herd. But I wanted to cook him something that would last a while. I didn't want him to go hungry.

Sneaking out of the tent was difficult with the crutches, but I guessed I wore him out the night prior, because he didn't stir. My face flushed in remembrance of our time together. Being inside of Verus was like a dream. I warred with myself on whether it was better to wake him with sex, but my need to feed him won out, and I hobbled away, keeping the weight on my good leg.

The sun had yet to come up, the sky only just turning gray, so most of the village was quiet. I saw a few warriors who guarded the village at night marching around, but none approached me. I slipped into the cooking tent, already running through the ingredients in my head that I needed to make the treat for Verus. If I made enough, it could be shared with all the hunters who were going.

"What do you think you're doing?" a familiar voice snarled.

Jerking around almost sent me toppling to the ground, and the twist was painful on my injured leg. I grimaced, shifting my weight to take the edge off the pain.

"You are planning to do something to the food, aren't you?" Saneth accused. "I knew it was a trap to trust you."

My brows furrowed. "What would I do to the food? I am here to cook."

He didn't look like he believed me, his eyes narrowed and suspicious. "Arms out. I will find the poison on you and prove it."

Looking down at the crutches and back at him, I wasn't sure exactly what he wanted me to do. If I put my arms out, the crutches would fall, and then so would I. He seemed to come to the same conclusion because he made an irritated sound and stomped up to me, grabbing a stool nearby and shoving me onto it.

I stayed stiff as he searched my pockets, and he could only do it while I was seated because of the trousers that were made for me were so loose. His accusations were baseless—I would never do something so awful to the clan—but I was only a visitor here. If it came down to my word against his, the clan would no doubt choose to believe him. It reminded me too much of when Richard tricked me. I wanted to run away, to call for Verus, but I sat there frozen until Saneth had finished his search and stepped back again.

"You carry nothing on you," he complained.

I nodded slowly. "It's hard to reach my pockets with the crutches."

He glanced at the crutches, then back at me. He looked confused, his expression twisted. "Then why are you here if you are not planning to cause trouble?"

"Verus is going on a hunt," I explained, my voice trembling. "I was going to make him bread to take with him. If he's careful with it, it will last a while."

My answer seemed to surprise him. He studied me, looking for a lie, and when he didn't find one, he threw his hands up in frustration. "He said you were poisoning him!"

I didn't need to ask who. Tavik didn't like me, and it seemed like he wasn't above spreading rumors. I sank a little in on myself, fighting back tears. That kind of rumor would get me thrown out or even killed. I was terrified of what Saneth would do to me.

"I-I haven't. I swear."

Saneth growled and stomped away, spinning on his heel to march back. He did that several times, pacing in the tent, and when he came back again, his expression was more hesitant.

"I told him I'd catch you in the act. I've been watching you. But you are never alone. Not until now. Are you cooking the clan meal as well? Is that how you poison him?"

Shaking my head rapidly, I told him, "I can't cook for the clan yet. Yamileth would be angry with me. It's her job to feed the clan. I only help her."

His eyes flicked around the tent before narrowing on me again. "I don't believe you. We will bring you to Orthorr, see what he thinks."

"You will do no such thing." Yamileth's voice cut through the quiet, low and ominous. "It is not Patrick you should worry about. I'm the one who punished Tavik. Had he kept his mouth shut, he would not be suffering right now."

My mouth fell open at her confession. Even Saneth looked stunned, spinning around to face her.

"You punish him by poisoning him?" he screeched.

She scoffed. "No, I punish him by giving him the shits. Since his mouth is so full of shit, I felt it best to clear that from his system. Perhaps now he will speak better to others."

Saneth looked like he wasn't sure what to do with that information. Neither was I, for that matter. I watched as Yamileth elbowed him out of her way, coming to stand in front of me and cupping my face in her warm hands.

"Are you hurt?"

I shook my head minutely, grateful for her presence. "No. He let me sit down before questioning me."

She tsked, pinching my cheeks affectionately before releasing me. "At least he has some brains, then. Why are you here so early? You should be resting."

I glanced at Saneth, who still stood there gaping at her, but Yamileth seemed intent on ignoring him. "I, uh… Verus has to go on a long hunt. I was going to cook him and the other hunters some bread to bring with them so they don't get hungry."

She gifted me with a soft smile, patting my cheek again. "You're a good boy. I will help. If we add fruit, it will keep them healthy. A few of them use the long hunt to skip on their vegetables. Giant children, the lot of them."

I huffed out a laugh, still staring at her as she puttered around the tent, poking through the boxes of dried fruits and meats against one wall. She was quickly becoming my favorite person, aside from Verus. She cared more about me than my parents ever had.

She pointed me to my table where I prepped the bread daily and set me to work on mixing the ingredients. When she noticed Saneth still standing there, she rolled her eyes.

"Do you plan to stand there all day gaping like a fish?"

Her comment seemed to snap him out of his shock and he took a step back, pointing at her accusingly. "You admitted to a crime. I will be telling Orthorr."

"Do so," she challenged. "Perhaps he would like to know how you two treat our visitors. Or maybe he would like to hear of Tavik's intent to frame Patrick for a crime he did not commit. You two are not without fault. Now, begone. And don't come back. You two can feed yourselves for a while. Perhaps that will teach you some manners."

Saneth paled at her accusations, no longer looking like the tough barbarian warrior. Instead he resembled a little boy getting scolded by his grandmother. I'd laugh if the situation wasn't so upsetting. I was still afraid that he'd tell the clan leader that I was poisoning Tavik and get me thrown out.

His mouth gaped open and closed for a moment before he spun on his heel and hurried off. I watched him go with my heart in my throat, only turning back to my work when Yamileth put her hand on my shoulder.

"Do not have fear, Patrick. They got what they deserved. Though, next time I will add more visek to Saneth's meals. He should have been suffering alongside his little friend. He has a stronger gut than Tavik does."

Stunned, I whipped my head around to look at her. "So you were telling the truth? You really poisoned him?"

She scoffed, waving a wrinkled hand dismissively. "No. Visek is not fatal. It merely clears out the system. He would need to eat the whole bush to suffer anything more than the shits from it."

My stomach dropped out, and an incredulous laugh bubbled up in my throat. She grinned and winked at me, puttering away to grab the dried fruit for the bread.

"Have you done this before?" I had to ask.

She snickered, setting the dried fruit on my table. "On occasion. The clan knows better than to bite the hand that feeds them. If Tavik had been smart, he would have avoided my tent for a time after upsetting you. It is his own arrogance that landed him in his predicament."

I should have questioned her more when she said she'd handled them. I thought a little old woman wouldn't have been able to cause much trouble. I was very wrong. And now I knew better than to ever make her angry. I didn't want to face the same consequences as Tavik.

Hoping to stay on her good side, I quickly got to work, mixing the ingredients together and folding in the dried fruit. The dough went into a covered pot hanging over the fire. I hoped it would be done before Verus left. I'd lost time when Saneth came to harass me.

After stoking the fire, I moved to start the morning preparations for breakfast. It took time and planning to feed an entire village. It made me wonder how Yamileth handled it all by herself.

"Have you always worked alone?" I queried while chopping some fruit into small pieces. The toddlers would choke if I didn't.

She hummed, shaking her head. "Not always. My husband would help me when he was alive. My sons did while they were little, until they grew bored of it. A few in the clan offer their help, but you will see when they do that they only cause more work. It is not hard to chop things evenly. They ruin the food with such sloppiness."

I snickered, doling out the fruit into small bowls. "I'm glad I don't cause you trouble."

She stopped beside me, pinching my cheek again. "As am I, young one. Now enough chit chat. We have work to do."

A smile pulled at my lips as I followed her directions. My father always hated that I was more interested in cooking than things like fighting or hunting for sport. He thought it was an embarrassment, especially when I opened a bakery instead of a tavern. He thought at least a tavern wouldn't be considered women's work. But my skills were needed here. I was glad I followed my heart.

Nineteen

When I woke alone, I was disappointed and a little worried. Patrick and I woke together most days. I enjoyed spending quiet mornings with him, getting cleaned up by the river and getting him settled in the cooking tent. That he was not with me when I woke was concerning. I went looking for him, my worry compounding when I saw a group of people hovering around the cooking tent. Even from outside, I could hear the raised voices of Tavik and Yamileth. But where was Patrick?

Pushing my way through the crowd, I stepped into the tent. My eyes immediately landed on Patrick, who sat on a stool in his usual spot, his gaze locked on the trio speaking nearby. Yamileth stood with her arms crossed, her glare locked on Tavik, who was throwing a tantrum of epic proportions while Orthorr listened on. Coming in late, I didn't know the full situation, but what little I heard was surprising.

"She should be banished!" Tavik demanded.

Yamileth snorted, raising an eyebrow at him. "And who then would feed the clan?"

She had a point. Whatever she had done, it was unlikely that Orthorr would send her anywhere. She was necessary to the clan. No one else could cook like she could, especially not for such a large number of people. We had been spoiled for many years since she became the clan cook.

"No one is getting banished," Orthorr insisted, putting his hands up in a calming gesture. "Yami, will you tell me why—"

"It does not matter why!" Tavik bellowed. "She poisoned me!"

My mouth fell open in shock. "She what?"

All eyes swung to me. Ordinarily, joining in on clan matters without Orthorr's invitation would not be allowed. But Orthorr knew why I was here. He tipped his head toward Patrick, allowing me to move to Patrick's side to protect him in case Tavik did something stupid. Just in time too, since Tavik's focus swung Patrick's way once I got close to him. He jabbed a finger at Patrick, baring his teeth at him.

"This is your fault! You are so weak that you could not take a joke so you went crying to the elders and turned them against me! You should not even be here! You are not clan! Verus should have left you in the woods to the shadowstalker!"

Moving in front of Patrick protectively, I glared at Tavik. "Choose your next words carefully. You lie to save face. Your cruel words were no joke. You are right that Yami should not have been the one to deal with you. It is me you should have faced. I am more than happy to correct that error now."

I heard Patrick's gasp, felt his hand fist in the back of my tunic. He was worried for me, probably because Tavik was bigger than I was. That didn't matter. He was an idiot and not a good fighter. Rath's father taught me to fight well when we were boys. Rath and I still practiced together several times a week. I had no fear of Tavik.

"Enough," Orthorr barked. "Someone will explain to me what happened now, or you both will face the consequences."

Tavik opened his mouth, but Orthorr interrupted him with a glare. "Not you. You have said enough."

Orthorr's gaze shifted to me, silently demanding that I speak.

"Tavik called Patrick many cruel things, thinking he could get away with it because Patrick is not a tribute. Had I not had Patrick to protect, I would have handled it between us."

Tavik opened his mouth to argue with me, but a dark look from Orthorr made his jaw snap shut again. He knew better than to talk back to our clan leader. That could get you banished or demoted. He could be on trench duty for months for the insult alone.

"So you walked away to protect Patrick. Why then is Tavik accusing Yamileth of poisoning him?"

I did not have an answer for that. I hadn't known she intended to get involved. Had I known, I would have requested she not. She was getting older and frail, and Tavik was emotional when angry. I didn't want him lashing out and hurting her.

All eyes swung to Yamileth, who crossed her arms over her chest, her chin lifted in defiance. "He made Patrick cry. He deserved what he got."

Orthorr's sigh was long suffering when he asked, "What did you do exactly?"

"I added visek to his meals. If so much shit was coming from his mouth, I felt it necessary to give him assistance to clear it out. He is here complaining from embarrassment, not pain."

I couldn't help it. I burst out laughing. Visek was a healing herb, usually given in small amounts to clan members after a long hunt if they got backed up. If she laced his food with it, Tavik probably spent hours, or maybe even days at the trench dealing with the consequences. How long depended entirely on how many meals he got from her between now and when she began to torment him.

"Verus," Orthorr scolded, though I could see the way his lips twitched. He was fighting back his own laugh. Meanwhile, Tavik looked close to losing it. His face was bright red, and he looked ready to explode.

"This is not funny! You say I am cruel, and yet she can do things like this without consequences?" he snarled.

Clearing his throat, Orthorr shook his head. "No one said she would be without consequences. Yamileth, you will choose two others to help you and Patrick with the cooking. They will watch over you to make sure you aren't tampering with other people's meals."

Yamileth glowered, but didn't argue. She hated people in her cooking tent. She thought them bothers who would only get in her way. Only Patrick ever won her over enough to allow her to let him assist.

"Fine. But he is still not allowed back in here," she snapped, pointing an accusing finger at Tavik. "He sent his little cohort in here to accost Patrick. They do not deserve to be fed by the clan. They can feed themselves."

Orthorr's brows furrowed, and he turned to look at Tavik again. "Care to explain yourself?"

I wanted him to speak up too. I felt the distinct urge to go hunting for Saneth for such actions.

Tavik refused to speak, his lips pressed together in a thin line. That got him a dark look from Orthorr, but he didn't waste his time demanding it. Instead he turned to Patrick, still mostly hidden behind me.

"Verus, move so I can see him."

Reluctantly, I side stepped to give Orthorr room to see my ravsol without moving from the path between Tavik and Patrick. I still didn't trust him. Patrick looked worried, his hand still clinging to my tunic and his body hunched in on itself. Like he was afraid he would be hurt. I took his free hand and kissed the back of it.

"You are safe, my Patrick. Tell Orthorr what happened."

Patrick's hand tightened in mine, and I could see his gaze dart to the tent flap. He wanted to run away. But when his gaze returned to me, he shored up his courage and drew in a deep breath, forcing himself to look up at Orthorr.

"I woke early this morning to come here. I hoped to cook something for Verus before he left on the long hunt. I hadn't even begun when Saneth joined me. He accused me of causing trouble and poisoning Tavik. He said he was going to prove it, but when he searched me and found nothing on me, he—"

"He touched you?" I snarled, launching to my feet. I fully intended to go after Saneth for even looking at Patrick, but Orthorr put a hand on my shoulder, shoving me back down.

"Do not leave Patrick while he is frightened because of bloodlust," Orthorr ordered. "Keep going, Patrick. What happened next?"

Patrick looked worriedly at Yamileth, who shook her head. "Tell him, Patrick. He knows already that I am responsible for Tavik's punishment."

"It was not a punishment!" Tavik shouted. "It was poisoning! I did nothing to deserve it! It is not my fault he is—"

He did not have time to finish his sentence before I lunged at him, tackling him to the ground. I would not allow him to say one more insult toward Patrick. No one was allowed to hurt my ravsol.

I only got two good punches in before Tavik came out of his shocked stupor and fought back. His meaty fist hit my jaw, sending me sprawling, but I was quick to recover, grabbing the arm that reached for me and twisting it behind his back. I was shoving his face into the dirt floor when two brothers who had been watching just outside grabbed me, hauling me off of Tavik. Two more stopped him before he could come after me again, holding him back with dark looks in their eyes. Should he keep pushing, they would lay him out without issue. I could only wish that he would test them. It would be a glory to watch.

"Remove them both," Orthorr ordered. "I will speak to Patrick alone."

Shaking off the hold of my brothers, I stomped out, stopping alongside Rath who stood near the entrance. "Watch over him," I requested under my breath.

Rath dipped his chin once, slipping into the cooking tent with Finn following behind him. If I could trust anyone to watch over Patrick, it was Rath. He would keep Patrick safe until I could get to him again. In the meantime, I would make sure no one else was stupid enough to speak ill of him again.

Twenty

Nothing this morning was going as I had planned. What was supposed to be a nice gesture to make something for Verus to bring along on his journey ended up being a battle with me caught in the middle. I could only watch helplessly as Verus and Tavik rolled on the ground, punching each other. It took four barbarians to pull them apart, and from the look on Verus's face, he wasn't done yet. He only walked away because Orthorr demanded it.

A hand on my shoulder startled me, and I looked up to see Finn hovering at my side, a worried frown tugging at his lips. "Are you okay?"

My smile was more of a grimace. "I'm alright. Verus?"

"He will be fine," Rath grunted from where he stood nearby, his arms crossed over his wide chest. He was an intimidating sight, but his scowl wasn't directed at me. It was aimed at the tent flap, where a few faces peeked in, like he was daring anyone to get close to me. It was kind of nice, knowing someone was willing to protect me when Verus wasn't around.

A barbarian I wasn't familiar with ordered the group to disperse before joining us in the cooking tent. It was getting a little crowded in here, and no work could be done with all the chaos. Yamileth ignored it all, puttering around to check on the bread we'd made earlier. I was glad she hadn't forgotten about it. It would've made this whole thing worse if the reason I was wandering around alone ended up being ruined.

For a long moment, the two barbarians spoke with one another, their words too fast for me to follow. When I glanced at Finn, even he was frowning, like he couldn't quite keep up. He had only been with the clan for a few months. It wasn't really surprising that he struggled when people were speaking quiet and quick like they were.

When they finally turned around to face me, their expressions were stoic, and I felt myself shrink away from them automatically. Finn rubbed my shoulder reassuringly, and I was grateful that he stayed by my side when the clan leader and the unknown barbarian stepped up to me.

"Patrick, this is Uttin. He is head of the warriors who protect our clan, including Tavik and Saneth. I would like him to hear your story again. Start from the beginning, please. From your first interaction with Tavik."

It didn't really feel like I had any other choice, so I started with the confrontation at the river and went up to this morning, when Saneth accused me of poisoning Tavik. By the time I was done, I was bright red with shame and embarrassment, and I couldn't look the two men standing over me in the eye.

"I'm sorry. I didn't mean to cause so much trouble."

Yamileth made an irritated noise, coming to stand by my other side. "What trouble did you cause? Existing? You did nothing to either of them. They are the ones acting like children."

"She's right," Uttin agreed. "You have nothing to apologize for. It is we who need to apologize for your ill treatment. You are a guest in our clan and should not have been treated as such. I will speak with them both and make sure it doesn't happen again."

I jerked my head up, horrified at the prospect. From my experience, calling out a bully only made things worse. But who was I to argue with them? As Tavik said, I wasn't part of the clan. I didn't have a say.

"Um…"

Finn's quiet voice caught the clan leader's attention, and he turned to look at him, his expression soft for the shy man. "Finn? Do you have something to say?"

Finn bit his lip, shifting uncomfortably under Orthorr's gaze. He only felt comfortable to speak when his bondmate stepped up behind him, putting his hand on Finn's shoulder.

"I, um… I've had experience with men like Tavik. It's possible that calling him out will only make things worse for Patrick. He's already resentful. I don't want him to get hurt."

Orthorr gave him a soft smile, dipping his chin to acknowledge him. "We will take that into account. I assure you, Patrick is safe here. He is our guest, and I will not allow him to come to harm. Should Tavik or Saneth approach him again, the consequences will be severe."

I wasn't sure that would be enough, especially once Verus left. I almost wanted to ask that he stay behind. I felt safe with him. I wasn't sure how I'd feel once he was gone.

◈

I WENT AS FAR AS PAST THE VILLAGE CENTER BEFORE I SWUNG AROUND TO face Tavik. He shook off the brothers holding him, squaring up to me with his chin lifted. No words needed to be said. Our fight was unfinished. I would not leave to hunt until Tavik was put in his place. Fellow brothers stood watch to make sure we didn't kill each other, but they understood the need for violence. To once and for all put this to bed.

He lunged at me, always so predictable, and I ducked as he swung, aiming for his gut instead. It winded him, and he stumbled but recovered quickly enough. His hand flung out, grabbing my tunic to drag me closer, but I used the momentum to strike just under his jaw. His teeth clacked together from the force, and he had to release me as he fought to shake off the stunning blow.

I tried to go low again, since he tended to strike high, used to only fighting people who matched his size, but he saw it coming and spun, catching me in a headlock.

"You see? I am better than that casak fawning all over you. I am not so pathetic to be chased from my home."

His words against Patrick only enflamed me more. Twisting my head, I shoved his face with my free hand, forcing him to release me. I grabbed the arm that had been around my head, forcing it behind his back, and kicked out his knee. He dropped to the ground with a shout, landing heavily on his chest. Kneeling on his back, I hissed, "Patrick is ten times the man you are. He makes me happy. Should he claim me, I will bond with him."

"But he... is not... clan..." Tavik gritted out.

"No. But if he chooses to leave, I will go with him. That is how much I care for him." Shoving away from him, I took a step back. "Give up, Tavik. I have found my bondmate. I will never be interested in you."

To my surprise, he didn't jump to his feet or try to attack again. I waited for it, but he stayed on the ground, his body limp in defeat.

"Walk away," Feigrind, who had stood watch during the fight, urged me, putting a hand on my shoulder and pushing me gently toward the village center. "He understands now. No need to rub it in his face."

I waited a second more to make sure Tavik wouldn't do something stupid like claim I was a coward for walking away before stomping off. I couldn't go back to Patrick, not until Orthorr was done speaking to him, but that didn't mean I wouldn't stay nearby. My Patrick was frightened earlier. I wanted to be there to comfort him when their conversation was through. I also wanted to make sure he wasn't blamed for any of it. He was not at fault. The problems lay with me and Tavik.

It took time for Orthorr and Uttin to leave the cooking tent. While I waited, I paced outside, ignoring the stares and whispers from my fellow clan members. I only stopped when they stepped out, waiting warily for them to speak.

Orthorr waved toward the tent. "He's fine, but I'm sure you wish to check on him anyway. Go."

Needing no further encouragement, I hurried inside the tent, heading straight for Patrick. He was on his usual stool, his face clouded with worry. I hated it. He needed to always be smiling. I wished I could add more bruises to Tavik for putting that look on his face.

Rath noticed my arrival and gently tugged Finn's elbow, pulling him away from Patrick's side. He nodded at me in acknowledgement and left, giving me the space to talk to Patrick alone.

"Do not distract him long. He has work to do," Yami warned.

Well, mostly alone. And despite her grouchiness, I knew she wouldn't stop me from comforting Patrick. His gaze lifted, and he chewed his lip, unhappiness coming off him in waves. Kneeling in front of him, I cupped his cheek, resting my forehead against his.

"He won't come near you again, my Patrick. I promise."

Pushing forward until his face was buried against my shoulder, he clung to me. I wrapped myself around him, giving him all the support and love I could offer. It frustrated me that he'd struggled so much since arriving here. I wanted better for him. And now I would be forced to leave his side for an indeterminate amount of time. It felt a little as though the fates were fighting against us. It would break my heart if that was true. I wanted to dedicate the rest of my life to Patrick. He was my perfect match. I would do insane things to keep him by my side. Including going against the fates.

Twenty-One

Even though I wanted him to stay, I didn't ask Verus to not go on the hunt. I couldn't. It was his job, and he'd told me how honored he was to serve his clan. Instead, I forced a smile and wrapped up the bread I'd made for him and the three others who were going on the hunt. When I handed it to him, he looked at the bundle curiously, tipping his head at me.

"What's this?"

I was so hopelessly smitten with him, I could only shrug helplessly and blush as I admitted, "I wanted you to have enough to eat. If you're careful, it should last a while. Yamileth added some fruit to it, so it's healthy and—"

He swooped down, cutting me off with a kiss that took my breath away. It was so intense and filled with emotions that I didn't dare hope for, I could only cling to him and try to commit the feeling to memory. When he pulled away, resting his forehead against mine, I felt a lump form in my throat.

"I won't be gone long, ravsol. The others will face Rath if they drag their feet. He will not allow it to take longer than necessary."

As much as I wanted him to hurry, I didn't want him putting himself at risk either. "Be safe," I pleaded, my fingers digging into his tunic. I'd just found him. I couldn't stomach the thought of losing him.

Smiling softly, he rubbed his forehead against mine in an affectionate gesture. I closed my eyes and savored it, and when he was summoned to join the other hunters, I firmed up my resolve and forced myself to smile for him.

"Go. Do your duty for the clan. I'll be here when you get back."

He stole one last kiss before pushing to his feet and walking out of the cooking tent. A part of me didn't want to watch him go, but I couldn't help but follow, hobbling on my crutches to see him off.

Finn was in a similar state about Rath's departure. Tears streamed down his cheeks, and he clung to Rath's tunic until Zoya pulled him away. Moving to stand beside him, I nudged him to get his attention.

"They'll be okay as long as they're together. Right?"

Sniffling, Finn looked up at his bondmate, then at Verus, who was on his horse beside Rath, his expression serious. Finn huffed out a watery laugh at that expression, shaking his head.

"He's never that serious. It looks weird."

A smile tugged at my lips and I tipped my head, studying the barbarian I was falling for. "Maybe you're right. It looks wrong for him to be serious."

Verus, noticing he was the center of attention, frowned, looking between us. "What?"

Zoya smirked, rolling her eyes. "They think you look weird being all frowny like that. Lighten up a little. I'll watch over them."

Verus's expression softened, and he nodded once. "I trust you, clan healer. And Finn? I'll bring him back in one piece after proving I'm the better hunter. It won't take that long."

Rath rolled his eyes, but Verus's teasing did a lot to ease the heart-heavy feeling in the air. He winked at me, all smiles, and I forced my sadness away for him. I didn't want him out there worrying about me. I wanted him to focus on his task so he could come home safe.

"Move out," Rath grumbled, giving his bondmate one last soft look before turning his giant horse and making a clicking sound to get the animal moving.

The barbarians didn't start moving at an easy pace. He raced off at a gallop, the rest of the hunters following after him. Verus turned to look over his shoulder at me, lifting a hand to wave just before they all disappeared over a hill.

Finn choked on a sob, hugging his middle, and Zoya sighed, wrapping her arms around him. She flashed me a small smile.

"Are you okay?"

A part of me wanted to cry like Finn, but I held it back. "Yeah, I'm okay. Will he be okay?"

Poor Finn looked devastated and almost inconsolable. Zoya cuddled him close, kissing the top of his head affectionately. "He'll be alright. He just needs a distraction."

I thought about it for a moment, then tipped my head toward the cooking tent. "Finn? Do you want to help me with breakfast? I could use a hand." And technically, there were supposed to be two extra people in the tent to watch over Yamileth. She'd be a lot happier if one of them was Finn. He wouldn't get in her way.

Finn didn't immediately answer, but Zoya nudged him to get him moving, urging him along. "Come on. You can help Patrick while I check on Marienne. Her baby is due soon, and she said she didn't feel well this morning."

It took some coaxing, but eventually, I had Finn on a stool next to mine, carefully chopping vegetables. Yamileth didn't comment on his sad state, but she did put some tea in front of him, and every time she passed by, she patted his shoulder or touched his head to remind him she was there. It was sweet, but I got the feeling if I told anyone she was doing it, she'd adamantly deny it. The look she gave me when I smiled as she passed said she wouldn't appreciate me sharing the moment.

I was checking on the vegetables cooking in the pot above the fire when my favorite group of people joined us. A group of boys, from age two to ten, all came rushing in, begging for treats. They showed up every morning after breakfast, giving me and Yamileth big pleading eyes for more of their favorites. They found out pretty quickly that I was faster to give in than Yamileth was.

"Patrick!" they squealed, running up to me. I bit back a grin, pretending not to hear them, even while I sat back at my table and started chopping fruits for their treats. Little fingers pulled at my tunic, demanding my focus, and when I finally turned to look at them, they shoved the smallest right up front and nudged him.

"Do it!" his older brother whispered.

Taking his cue, the toddler put his hands together and stuck out his bottom lip, his eyes wide and pleading. "I has tweat?"

"Oh goddess, how can you say no?" Finn murmured, a crooked smile on his lips.

The other kids joined in, giving their biggest puppy dog eyes. "Please! Please, Patrick!"

Laughing, I nodded. "Fetch me your bowls, and you can each have more."

They squealed and raced off to get the bowls, all but the youngest, who didn't have a hope of keeping up. I snatched him before he could toddle off, pulling him into my lap and handing him a cut up piece of fruit.

Finn melted watching him, his red rimmed eyes finally dry. I introduced them, chuckling when the toddler asked Finn for more fruit instead of saying hello. He was happy to oblige the tot, offering him some from the pile I'd cut up.

"Will you take him? I need to get the rest of the fruit ready for the others."

Finn looked surprised but pleased when I handed him the toddler before I pushed to my feet to grab more fruit to cut up. Yamileth poked me in the side as I filled a small bag, rolling her eyes at me. "You're worse than I am."

I snickered, shaking my head. "I like kids. They never judged me or treated me badly. As long as I had bread and treats at my store, they were always happy to see me."

She hummed, patting my cheek affectionately. "You will make a good father someday. Verus is very lucky."

My cheeks flushed bright red at the thought of having children with Verus. I'd always thought about adopting when I got more settled. It got lonely in the store by myself, and there were kids out there who needed homes. Sharing that experience with Verus filled me with so much want, it made my chest ache.

"Do you think he'd want that?" I murmured. "With me, I mean?"

She rolled her eyes, a smile pulling at her lips. "I think if you told him you picked him, he'd bond with you before daybreak. Have you not noticed how he looks at you?"

Lifting a shoulder, I carried the bag back to my table and got comfortable on my stool again. "I want it to be real, but we've never discussed it. He's a sweet person in general. It could just be in his nature to dote on those he's... spending time with."

Finn snorted, raising his eyebrows at me. "You mean Verus? He's smitten with you. Rath says he's too distracted on the hunt because he won't stop thinking about you. I'm glad he went on the long hunt. He'll be just as eager to come back as Rath, and between the two of them, hopefully it won't take very long."

I hoped that too. Verus said he'd get back as soon as he could. Counting down the days was going to be brutal, though.

The children came back in a flurry, holding up their bowls for treats. I had to focus on cutting up the fruits and passing them out, struggling to keep up before their bowls were empty again, and they were begging for more. Yamileth had to eventually send them away to give me a break.

"Shoo! Off with you! You're going to eat all our food, and we'll have none for later! Wait until your next meal!"

They squealed and laughed, running from her as she batted at them with a towel. She chuckled as they disappeared, the last one being the toddler who slipped off Finn's lap to run after the others.

I sighed watching them go. If what she and Finn were saying was true, I could finally have the future I wanted. A future filled with love and warmth, with days feeding people and making them happy and nights wrapped in the arms of the man I loved. It was a dream I thought was too far-fetched to ever come true. But because of one barbarian who showed up to rescue me, maybe it could actually happen.

As soon as he came home, I'd ask. I had to. I needed to know one way or another if it was possible. Because the more time I spent with Verus, the harder I fell for him. If I had any chance of sparing myself the heartbreak, I needed to know sooner rather than later. Because I wanted forever with him. Hopefully, he wanted the same thing.

Twenty-Two

It took a week just to get close to the herd. A series of storms slowed us down while the herd moved farther south when the ground got too muddy for them to find food. With each passing day, I grew more frustrated. I'd promised Patrick I would be back quickly. If it took this long just to find the herd, it did not bode well for returning soon.

Rath ducked into our makeshift shelter, his long hair soaked and his expression annoyed. I sighed heavily.

"It's not going away any time soon, is it?"

He shook his head, sitting in front of the small fire. The others were just as unhappy about it, if the grumbles were anything to go by. Since the mud slowed us down just as much as the herd, we never hunted them during this kind of weather. But that just meant we were stuck here waiting until it passed.

"Do you think I am cursed?"

Rath looked up, his brow furrowed tightly in a frown. "What? Why would you ask this?"

I waved my hands wildly, my words rushed and frustrated. "Ever since I found Patrick, things have been difficult. I was not quick enough to find him before his injury, I scared him when we first met, and I could not protect him from Tavik's hurtful words. Yami had to step in because I was too distracted to deal with it myself. Orthorr still has yet to agree to let me bond with Patrick, and should he not allow it, I will be forced to leave my clan. And now all this." I thrust a hand at the storm outside our shelter, which answered back with a flash of lightning. I scowled. "We cannot go home until we get Morak what he needs, but the storm started the day we left. It feels as though I am cursed."

"Do you think Patrick is cursed, and it transferred to you?" Rhos suggested.

Horrified, I whipped my head around to look at him. "Why do you think that he's cursed?"

He lifted a shoulder from where he lounged on his bed roll, ticking off things on his fingers. "He was chased from his home, got lost in the forest, was hunted by a shadowstalker, and hurt himself so badly he cannot walk —all before he even met you. It sounds to me like he is more likely the one who is cursed, not you."

Rath made a *tsk* sound behind his teeth. "No one is cursed. I thought the same thing when Finn arrived. He has been fine since our bonding. It will pass."

Orvak, who sat near the entrance to the shelter as a lookout, glanced over his shoulder at us. "Perhaps it is all townsfolk who are cursed. You said Finn has been fine since the bonding. Maybe once he became a clan brother, the curse was broken."

Pursing my lips thoughtfully, I considered it. A lot of what happened did revolve around Patrick. I didn't want to consider the idea of him being cursed because it would only worry me more, being so far from him. But if Orvak was right, there was an easy fix for Patrick's problem. I needed only to bond with him to keep him safe.

Of course, that was easier said than done. I still hadn't gotten Orthorr's permission to bond with Patrick. I hadn't even asked Patrick if that was what he wanted. I felt like he would agree—he seemed happy with me— but a part of me was afraid to ask. What if he said no?

Rhos sat up, scowling at the rain. "I'm hungry. Whose turn is it to hunt dinner?"

We'd run out of the bread Patrick made us days ago. He'd mentioned that it would last if we were careful with it, but it was so delicious, it was too much to resist. My brothers and I were already planning on asking Patrick for more for our next hunt. I regretted being so gluttonous when we first set out. It would make me feel better if I had a little more of it right now.

"Verus and I will go," Rath grunted.

I didn't argue with him. Perhaps hunting would get my mind off of everything. There was nothing I could do about curses or the like right now, anyway. Not until I got back to Patrick.

Since the herd was in the plains, it was a journey to get to the closest forest for hunting small game. We tried to make our shelter somewhere in between the forest and the herd, but we still needed our stallions to cross the distance safely. We had to be quick while lightning coursed through the sky so we didn't end up hurt, and it was faster to do that with stallions.

"Make haste, Dhellgas. The weather is against us."

The stallion grunted, none too pleased about being left out in the rain for so long. Their shelter was only large enough to keep their food and heads dry. I was a little worried he'd refuse to hunt for the insult.

"I'll make it up to you once we're home," I promised him. I was going to make it up to Patrick when I got back, as well.

With an irritated toss of his head, Dhellgas followed Rath's stallion into a gallop towards the trees. The rain pelted my skin, cold and sharp, but I did my best to ignore it. I would only be more miserable if I focused on it.

We made it to the trees in record time, and I jumped off Dhellgas's back and patted his side as Rath and I drew our bows. I got a nip as he walked off, but I didn't comment on it. He was allowed to be annoyed. I knew I was.

It didn't take long to find some evrach enjoying a meal. With the sound of the rain silencing my footsteps, I was practically upon them when I finally let loose my arrow. Rath did at the same time, killing two in quick succession. The ease of that hunt surprised me, and I shot a look at Rath, who looked just as surprised.

"Perhaps we should reconsider hunting in the rain?" I suggested.

He huffed, reaching for the evrach and twisting its neck roughly to ensure it was dead. "Let's discuss it with the others. If it means we can get back sooner, I'm all for it, but not while lightning is in the air. It is too much of a risk."

True, but the lightning wasn't all the time. And mud or not, I could catch the coiwak. It might even mean we could catch more than one at the same time.

∼

"Patrick?"

Glancing over my shoulder, I smiled at Finn, beckoning him inside. It was just me in the cooking tent. Yamileth's bones didn't handle the poor weather well, and after I'd proved I could cook enough for everyone, she finally took some time to rest. I was slow-roasting some meat for our supper, and I mostly stayed in the cooking tent to avoid Verus's. It made me sad to be in there all alone.

Finn pulled off his cloak, wiping his face off on his tunic sleeve. He'd hovered around me and Zoya since Rath left, too heartbroken to be left alone for long. I liked his company, so I never said no to his visits, gesturing to an empty stool for him to join me. I handed him a basket of beans to prepare, giving his hands something to do while we sat out the storm.

"Does it always rain this much in this area?" he finally asked, leaning a little closer to the fire to stay warm.

I hummed, adding another log to the fire. "In the spring, yes. Not where you're from?"

He shook his head. "I lived farther south, near Hartheim."

My eyebrows shot up in surprise. "The capital? I thought they didn't participate in the treaty."

He shrugged. "We were close to it but still far enough away that the capital refused to send soldiers to protect us. It took a few days to get me to the clan after I was volunteered. I didn't realize the weather would be so different in the north."

Honestly, neither had I. I'd never been south before. I didn't realize how close our town was to the barbarian's winter hunting grounds. Granted, the forest between here and the town was massive, and I spent days wandering around, but still. Only a forest stood between our town and the barbarians during the winter season. I wondered what the mayor would do with that information. He'd probably freak out.

Finn sank in on himself a little, his lips turned down in a deep frown. "Rath usually keeps me warm at night. Without him, it's hard to sleep. I'm always cold."

"I was going to ask," I admitted. Finn was tiny, with no body fat to keep him warm, and the tents didn't have fires in them yet, except for the healing and cooking tents. Even I was a little uncomfortable at night, and Verus had plenty of furs in there to keep me warm.

Looking around, I considered our options. "We could stay in here?" I suggested. "Yami might complain, but at least we'll be warm, and it would spare me from having to try to walk back to Verus's tent with so much mud around." I gestured to the crutches with a grimace. It was a pain to get through the muddy paths between the tents. I'd needed to request help twice already because I nearly slipped and fell just walking to the trench to relieve myself. If I could avoid it unless absolutely necessary, it felt like a win for me.

"Are you sure?" Finn asked, twisting his fingers anxiously.

"Why not? My home was above my shop in town. How is this any different?"

Twenty-Three

I was right that Yamileth complained when she found me and Finn sleeping in the cooking tent, but after seeing how upset Finn was and how much it helped him to sleep near the fire, she relented. She even decided to join us after a while, stating the fire felt good on her aching joints. I agreed with her on that, since my leg hurt unless I was close to the fire. It also made the nights a little easier to bear, having those two to chat with and knowing someone was close by.

The rain had died down to a drizzle when I had an unexpected visitor. Yamileth had gone to check on the new mother and her baby, and Finn went to visit Zoya, leaving me alone in the cooking tent for the first time in days. It wasn't close to a meal time, so I wasn't expecting anyone to come in. When someone cleared their throat near the entrance, it surprised me. I jumped and whipped my head around, pressing a hand to my chest.

"Goddess."

Saneth grimaced, his expression apologetic, which was strange for him. I was wary about being alone with him, and my eyes flicked to the entrance of the tent for a moment. I contemplated calling out for help or leaving, but he could stop me before I got very far, and I wasn't sure anyone would be able to hear me if I yelled. The rain kept people in their tents for the most part. There weren't that many people around to hear me.

"I haven't done anything," I said quickly, shrinking away from him a little.

He shook his head. "I know you haven't. Well, I assumed you hadn't. No one else complained about being sick, and Tavik and I haven't been eating the food you made. I'm not here about that."

"Then why are you here?" I asked, a small tremble in my voice. Did he purposely wait until I was alone? Would he hurt me before anyone could show up to help?

Scrubbing the back of his neck, he grimaced again, looking uncomfortable speaking with me. He didn't look angry or anything, like he had the last time he cornered me alone. But I didn't trust him one bit. Richard had played the kind act before, and it nearly got me killed. I wasn't going to give Saneth the benefit of the doubt. He hadn't earned that right.

"I was wondering if you planned on bonding with Verus."

My brows snapped together, and I studied him carefully. "Why?"

His lip twitched in a scowl, but he masked it, shaking his head. "It's not important. I—"

"I'm not answering unless you tell me why," I insisted. I didn't see why my bonding with Verus mattered to him unless he planned on doing something to fight it on Tavik's behalf. Would he hurt me if I said I wanted to? Or did he plan on interrupting the ceremony that Finn had told me about?

"Forget it," Saneth snapped, spinning around to leave.

He got as far as the opening of the tent before letting out a frustrated growl and turning back around. His glare wasn't reassuring in the slightest, but his explanation surprised me.

"Tavik won't give up on the idea of Verus. Not even after being bested in a brawl and Verus saying it will never happen between them. If you plan on bonding with Verus, maybe he will finally let it go and move on."

Stunned, I sat silently for a moment. I knew Tavik was interested in Verus. It was hard to miss with the comments he'd made before.

"Do you think it will make a difference?" I queried softly.

Saneth rolled his eyes, but his expression turned uncertain, and he frowned down at his feet like the answer was hidden in the dirt. "I don't know. Verus saying he intended to leave with you should you wish it should have been enough. It is clear he only has eyes for you. But Tavik still has not let it go. I'm unsure if anything will change his heart on the matter."

I wanted to be overjoyed about what Verus had apparently said, but my attention was stuck on the pain in Saneth's voice. I thought maybe he was just worried for his friend, but why would he be in pain just because Tavik wouldn't let Verus go? Unless…

"You like him, don't you?"

He made an irritated noise, glaring at me, and crossed his arms defensively over his chest. His lack of answer was answer enough for me, but my silence bothered him, and he growled in frustration.

"No. I don't like him. I love him. I always have. But he only has eyes for Verus."

I had to bite back a wince at that statement. I wasn't sure what was worse: having to live with the idea of never finding love, or being in love with someone you knew you couldn't have. I doubted it was a recent development; Yamileth had said that Saneth and Tavik were always together. The thought was a painful one.

"Does he know?" I asked uncertainly.

It felt weird to be discussing this with him after the way he had treated me, but it looked like he needed someone to talk to.

He shook his head, his expression clouded. "No. We have been friends since we were children. He only sees me this way."

Feeling awkward having him standing there while I sat, I gestured to the empty stool nearby. While he sat, I considered his words. I'd never had a relationship before Verus, so I wasn't sure how to handle it.

Finn arrived before I could come up with an idea, and he pulled up short when he noticed Saneth beside me. Saneth looked ready to bolt, but I felt bad for him. Finn had been in a relationship longer than I had. Maybe he could help.

"He's just here to talk," I reassured Finn, gesturing him closer. Looking at Saneth, I asked, "Do you mind if I share with him? He might have an idea of what to do."

Saneth didn't look happy about the idea, but his shoulders slumped in defeat, and he waved me on with a sigh. "Go on."

Finn looked confused, his gaze flicking between us and his head tipped slightly. "Share what?"

"Saneth has feelings for Tavik, but he says Tavik only sees him as a friend. I've never had a relationship before. Do you have any ideas about what he can do? Aside from me bonding with Verus. We haven't discussed that yet, so I don't want that to be the only plan. I'm not sure it will help."

"Um... It might," Finn agreed with a bob of his head. "Bondings are sacred. Tavik might not like it, but he'll have to respect it. He could be kicked out of the clan if he tries to get between the two of you."

I liked that my bonding with Verus was a foregone conclusion to both of them. It made me feel like I wasn't being silly having hope.

"So you do plan to bond?" Saneth demanded. "He will have to move on if you do."

I shrugged. "Maybe. I'd like to. But we haven't talked about it yet. And while Tavik might be forced to let go of Verus, that doesn't mean he will turn to you instead. Not unless you do something about it."

Saneth cringed at the thought, ducking his head. "I am afraid. He is my closest friend. I do not wish to lose him."

Most of my wariness of him melted away at that comment. Yes, he'd been a jerk before, but seeing him hurting and being honest with me went a long way to helping me forgive him. It was possible he only said those things to make Tavik happy. Lots of Richard's friends were like that. They didn't look at me twice when he wasn't around and only bullied me when he was present to hear it.

"So you haven't told him?" Finn asked.

I shook my head, answering for Saneth, who looked too dejected to answer. "He says Tavik only sees him as a friend."

Frowning thoughtfully, Finn gave his full focus to Saneth. "He might not have even considered it if you haven't said anything."

Saneth looked up at him, confused. "What do you mean?"

"I mean, if you've been friends a long time and you've never given him any clues that you are interested, then he might not have given it any thought. I read a romance book once with a similar situation. The main character and her love interest had been friends since they were toddlers. He never thought of her that way until it was time for her to enter society and she asked him to dance with her. He was secretly thinking of her that way all along, but because she never showed any interest, he pushed those thoughts aside to protect their friendship. Only when he realized they both were interested did he make a move."

I wasn't much of a reader, having spent most of my time when I was younger in the kitchen with the cook, but Finn definitely was. And if it worked out for the characters in the book, it was worth considering. People wouldn't enjoy books like that if it didn't make them want the same thing.

"But… What if he doesn't want me? He only has eyes for Verus, he's never even looked at me in such a way," Saneth argued.

He looked terrified at the thought of coming clean to Tavik, which I totally understood. I was nervous about asking Verus if he wanted to bond with me, and I knew he liked me. Saneth didn't have that kind of reassurance.

Finn didn't look comfortable answering that, but I could see what he was thinking written on his face.

"You have to decide if it's worth the risk. Would you rather stay friends and risk watching him fall in love with someone else, or would you rather try so you know for sure, and maybe get what you want?"

Twenty-Four

The plan worked better than I had hoped. Using the rain and the mud hid both our scents and the sound of our approach. It did make the hunt more difficult, crawling through the mud like that, since we couldn't see one another through the deluge to know if everyone was in position. We had a general sense of how long it would take each person, and I waited until I assumed we were all ready before shifting to my knees in the tall grass and aiming my arrow at the nearest coiwak. It was one of the larger ones, which meant it would likely need more than one arrow to take it down, but I was prepared for that. Rath talked me through it, and as long as I focused, I could hit it twice without issue.

Letting out a slow breath, I aimed at the coiwak's chest, right at its heart.

Please let this work.

Releasing the arrow, I quickly drew another without taking my eyes off the coiwak. It reared up when it was struck but stumbled immediately. I hoped it was a good sign but let loose another arrow just in case, this one striking the beast in the head. I jerked out another arrow, lining it up again, but the coiwak collapsed with a groan without running away.

Several thuds nearby made me think my brothers were successful as well, but I had no time to check. The noises startled the herd, but instead of running toward the open plains like they had been since we started watching them, they darted in my direction instead. A stampede of coiwak had me scrambling to get out of the way. If I was trampled, I would likely not survive.

A high-pitched whinny drew my focus, and Dhellgas came out of nowhere, rearing up and pawing at the air, forcing the herd to change directions. I ran for him, climbing quickly onto his back, and watched as the herd turned toward Orvak's direction instead. I worried for him and urged Dhellgas into motion, racing for him.

Stallions were faster than coiwak, but the herd was closer than I was. When I was close enough to see him clearly, he was trapped in the middle of the herd, fighting to keep his feet, and I worried about him getting knocked down. If he did, the likelihood of me finding him in time would be slim.

Thankfully, Orvak was quick on his feet and managed to dodge the coiwak until I could get to him.

"Orvak! Here!"

Throwing out my hand, I reached for him, clinging to Dhellgas's mane to keep me on his back. Orvak lunged for me, swinging himself onto the stallion's back just before we passed him by. We ran with the herd, slowing until the coiwak could pass by us and we could turn around.

Once out of danger, we both fought to catch our breath, the fear making us breathless. When I looked over my shoulder at him, we both burst out laughing, letting go of the excess energy of the situation.

"I'm glad you're both okay," Rath said blandly as he approached. Rhos was not far behind him, worry for his brother written in his eyes. He only settled when Orvak hopped down and gave him a back-slapping hug. Watching your twin nearly get trampled had to be terrifying. I was glad Dhellgas was quick to act.

Patting his neck, I leaned to murmur to him. "I owe you big time. I will tell Godr to pamper you when we get back. Once he finds out what you did, he'll likely give you all the treats."

That seemed to make the stallion happy, his head bobbing in agreement. Chuckling, I jumped down from his back, grunting when Rath pulled me into a tight hug. The action surprised me, and it took me a second to hug him back.

"Rath?"

"They turned in your direction first. Had your stallion not been there…"

Tightening my grip on him, I smiled to myself. This was just a reminder of how much I loved my clan. Rath was not my blood brother, but he was my family, and he cared that I was safe and well. It meant a great deal to me that we could hunt together like this.

With a final clap on my back, he released me, jerking his chin toward the coiwak who were taken down in the hunt.

"Let's see who was successful. Hopefully, we do not need to do this twice."

It was hard to see from a distance with the pouring rain how many were taken down. I knew that mine was, and I'd heard thumps that made me think I wasn't the only one who succeeded, but how many was a good question. Jogging down the hill, I tipped my head as we got closer.

"Three?"

I looked at the other hunters. Orvak and Rath both looked confused, so I doubted it was them who missed their shot, but when I glanced at Rhos, his face was flushed bright red. A slow grin pulled at my lips.

"Did you miss?"

"Not on purpose!" he grouched.

"Does one ever miss on purpose?" Orvak teased.

"What happened? Was the target too big?" I added with a smirk.

"Perhaps he needs more training," Rath commented, a mask of stoicism ruined by the way his eyes danced with mirth. "I thought he was ready for such a hunt."

Rhos groaned and dropped his head back, speaking to the skies instead of us. "Why must I be stuck with them? What did I do to deserve it?"

Laughing, I threw an arm around his shoulders, tugging him closer. "You love us. Do not pretend otherwise."

He put up with more teasing while we prepared the dead coiwak to move. They were too large to tie to the stallions' backs, so we'd brought a cart with us for the journey home. Rhos was assigned to draw the cart, since he missed his shot, but he was good natured about it, and his mount, a sweet and patient stallion, never seemed to mind pulling the extra weight.

"Luckily for you, Verus's kill is large enough to cover your mistake," Rath commented as we loaded the coiwak into the cart. Mine was so heavy, it took both of us to lift it.

Jerking my head around, I eyed him hopefully. "Does that mean what I think it does?"

Rath dipped his chin once, a slow smile spreading across his face. "I believe this is enough for Morak. It is time for us to go home."

Relief and excitement exploded in me, and I couldn't help but let out a whoop, thrusting my fist into the air. Finally, I would return to my Patrick. And once we were together again, I was going to ask him to bond with me. Orthorr would have to accept it, or we would leave once Patrick was able, but I would not go another day without Patrick knowing who he was to me.

IT TOOK A LOT OF ENCOURAGEMENT, AND SEVERAL DAYS OF CONVERSATION, to convince Saneth that speaking with Tavik was the best plan of action. We offered him other ideas at first, since he seemed so against it, but none seemed good enough for him. It wasn't until Yamileth found out why he was visiting that he was convinced, and only after she fed him two cups of very strong barbarian alcohol.

"I can't have a full cup by myself," Finn murmured, watching Saneth drain his second cup. "It only takes half to get me drunk. Any more and I'll pass out. I don't know how he can manage two."

Snickering, I shook my head. Yamileth offered me some, but while I was no longer in the splint, I still needed a cane to walk and didn't want to mess with my balance by drinking.

Saneth set his cup down with a thunk, his face screwed up in drunken determination. "Okay. Let's do this."

Yamileth rolled her eyes. "We will not be joining you. This is a conversation between the two of you."

I'd never seen Saneth pout before, but it was a little hilarious seeing such a tough barbarian stick out his bottom lip like that. Finn had to hide his laughter behind his hand, his shoulders shaking with the effort.

"But what if he hates me?"

"Then come back here and I'll give you more ale," Yamileth offered, waving him toward the entrance. "Now go before the storm starts again."

The rain hadn't stopped, but it was more of a heavy drizzle now, and there was no more lightning. I looked forward to when the weather changed, but spring rain lasted at least a month. We had a few weeks left.

With a whine, Saneth got to his feet, listing a little from the alcohol in his system. I steadied him with a hand on his arm, and Yamileth gave him a little push toward the tent flap. She followed him and watched him walk away before waving us closer.

"Come."

"Where are we going?" I asked as I followed her, leaning heavily on my cane. The rain had made my leg ache since I'd hurt myself.

"We can't hear them from here. He went around the bend. We need to get closer."

"We're going to eavesdrop?" Finn whispered harshly, even while he followed us both out of the cooking tent and in the direction Saneth had wandered off.

"Of course we are," Yamileth chastised him. "Do you wish to miss it?"

I bit back a snicker, following close behind them. While eavesdropping on a private moment felt a little wrong, I couldn't resist going along. I wanted it to work out for Saneth. In the past few days of talking to each other, he'd proved himself to be a nice guy. Head over heels for Tavik, which made him a little rash in how he acted, but he did apologize for the way he treated me. I liked him a lot, and I hoped he would find his happy ending.

We heard the conversation before we saw them. At least we heard Tavik while he ranted. I wasn't sure if Saneth had even gotten a word in edgewise with the way Tavik was going off, and when we peeked around the nearest tent, Tavik was pacing and throwing his hands up to emphasize himself.

"I mean, what does he see in that casak? I am a warrior for the clan!"

Tuning out his ranting words, I murmured to Finn, "What does casak mean?"

He winced. "It's a not nice term for outsider."

I tried not to roll my eyes. Tavik was focusing on something I knew in my soul that Verus didn't care about. He didn't care that I was from one of the towns. Most of the clan didn't. Tributes were from the towns. They'd lose their way of life if they didn't invite outsiders in.

"Tavik," Saneth called out, trying to interrupt him. Tavik wasn't listening, still ranting.

"He is making a mistake! Once he makes the bond, he will be stuck! I need to convince him before he ruins everything!"

"Tavik!" Saneth tried again. I watched in wide-eyed fascination as calm Saneth lost his temper, stepping in front of Tavik and shoving his shoulder hard. "Let him go! He has no interest in you! You are blind to not see it! You are blind to everything!"

Tavik looked stunned, taking a step back from his friend. "Saneth?"

Saneth shook his head roughly, glaring up at Tavik. "Your obsession with him is pathetic. He has never been interested, and you have wanted him for years."

That probably wasn't the way he wanted to start this conversation. I wished I could step in to stop him. The alcohol was probably loosening his tongue quite a bit, but if I came out of hiding, I would only draw Tavik's attention and start his rant all over again. At least now, Saneth had his attention with his harsh words.

"I am not blind," Tavik said defensively.

"You are," Saneth growled. "I have been in front of you, loving you, for years, and you do not notice. You are too obsessed with what you cannot have." Huffing out a derisive laugh, he shook his head. "I am no better for obsessing over you. No longer, Tavik. If you cannot let him go, then I cannot stand by you anymore. He has chosen another. Have honor and accept it."

Twenty-Five

I sucked in a breath as Saneth turned on his heel to storm off, worried Tavik would let him, but was relieved when Tavik lurched forward, grabbing Saneth's arm.

"What are you talking about? You love me?"

I wasn't sure if it was my own hopeless romantic ideas that made me think Tavik sounded hopeful. I was glued to the confrontation, hanging on their every word as Saneth bared his soul to the man he loved.

"I have loved you every day since we were seventeen. I have pined for you, wished for you to notice me. You never did. I understand I am nowhere as pretty as Verus or any of the others you chased since you came of age. But I still hoped you would notice me anyway."

Tavik looked blown away by the confession, his eyes wide. "I did not know…"

"And now that you do?" Saneth demanded, lifting his chin and facing Tavik head on. "Does it change anything?"

I felt my breath catch in my throat as I waited for Tavik to respond. Finn grasped my hand tightly, watching just as avidly as I was. I pleaded in my head for Tavik to say something, but as the silence stretched on, I could see the hope die in Saneth's eyes. He gently pushed Tavik's hand off his arm, taking another step back.

"It's okay. I understand. I'm sorry."

My heart broke for him as he turned again to walk away. I was going to leave, go back to the cooking tent so I could be there if Saneth came to talk, but Finn's grip tightened on my hand, and I turned around just in time to watch Tavik lunge forward, spinning Saneth around and capturing his lips in a passionate kiss.

Finn let out a little squeak, practically bouncing with joy. Yamileth looked smug on my other side, winking at me when I raised my eyebrow at her. A part of me wanted to cheer for them both. I was grateful that I held Finn's hand and my cane to keep myself from doing something so embarrassing. But still, it felt like something to celebrate.

"Woah. Maybe we should give them privacy," Finn murmured, his face flushing bright red.

I swung around to look at the couple again. My mouth fell open as Tavik pulled one of Saneth's legs around his hip, grinding against him. Yep, now was a good time to leave.

Yamileth batted my hand when I tried to pull her away. It took both me and Finn to make her move, and she complained the minute we were out of sight of the couple.

"It was just getting to the good part! If they wanted privacy, they would move to a tent!"

Snickering, I tugged her arm gently. "You do not truly wish to watch them doing that."

"Watch who doing what?"

My heart skipped at the familiar voice, and I looked up to find the man of my dreams standing just outside the cooking tent, a curious smile on his face.

"Rath!"

I barely noticed the flash of curly brown hair as Finn darted away from me. He launched himself at Rath, who was not far away from Verus, wrapping his arms and legs around his bondmate and peppering his face with kisses. Those kisses quickly turned steamy, and I felt my cheeks flush as I jerked my gaze away. For the second time in a day, I felt like I needed to walk away to give someone their privacy.

Yamileth chuckled beside me, patting my arm. "Go. I will handle supper tonight. I'll see you in the morning."

She didn't need to tell me twice. I closed the distance between me and Verus, who wrapped himself around me the second I was close enough. In that moment, I didn't feel the rain or the ache in my leg; I felt nothing other than the warmth of his body and the sense of belonging I'd craved my entire life. Wrapping one hand around the back of his neck, I tugged him down to kiss me, melting when he brushed light kisses against my lips, making my heart soar.

I wanted to drag him away to his tent, to give us some privacy to get reacquainted, but before I could convince myself to release his lips, someone cleared their throat to get our attention.

Verus growled, jerking his head up, then winced when he realized who it was. He stepped back only far enough to put a fist against his chest and bow his head respectfully. "I apologize, clan leader. Did you need something from me?"

Orthorr looked amused at least, not angry, as he tipped his head toward his tent. "Come speak with me. Bring Patrick with you."

Unease settled over me, and I clung to Verus's hand as we made our way to Orthorr's tent. It was larger than Verus's, with a section set up for speaking with people around a small table. We sat together on one side, with Orthorr across from us. Verus looked less worried than me, his focus on my leg as I settled beside him.

"The splint is gone."

"Zoya switched me to a cane yesterday," I explained, gaze darting between Verus and Orthorr. It felt weird to be talking so casually when the clan leader obviously wanted to speak to us.

"Does it still hurt?" Verus asked, leaning to put his hand on my leg where I was injured.

I tipped my head back and forth slightly. "A bit sometimes. If I do too much, it does. But it's better than before. And the cane helps."

"Zoya tells me he will keep improving with the poultices, as long as he doesn't overdo it. Patrick has been a great asset to the clan during these last few weeks, and we all wish for him to get better," Orthorr said with a smile.

Verus finally turned to face Orthorr, his brows drawn together. "Does that mean he can stay?"

Sucking in a breath, I jerked to face Orthorr. I had forgotten that it wasn't just Verus who decided if I got to stay. I was so focused on speaking with Verus, telling him how I felt about him, that I'd forgotten there were more obstacles between me and the future I wanted.

"I spoke with the elders, and had a runner speak with the clan leaders closest to us," Orthorr began. "It was decided that unless an outsider is brought in as a tribute, they cannot be allowed to join a clan."

My heart sank, and Verus looked ready to argue, but Orthorr put up a hand to stall us both. "Let me finish. While we aren't comfortable with just anyone joining the clan, Patrick is an exception. He has taken on a heavy burden for the clan and given Yamileth the chance to rest that she desperately needs."

Yamileth scoffed as she swept into the tent, glaring at Orthorr. "Desperate, my ass," she grouched. "No one was desperate."

Orthorr shot her an exasperated look, but Verus cut off her bickering before she could get us sidetracked. "So, what can we do? Do we need to name him a tribute?"

"No, a tribute was already accepted from Patrick's town this year," Orthorr said with a shake of his head. "We had another idea in mind. Yamileth actually suggested it, since she was the one benefiting the most from Patrick's assistance."

Frowning, I glanced over at Yamileth. Her normal scowl was missing, and her smile was soft as she cupped my face in her warm hands.

"You told me before that your family did not care for you. Should you accept, I would like to bring you into my family instead. You will be part of the clan through family, and can bond with whoever you wish."

My eyes widened so much, I felt like they would fall out of my head. "Y-you want to adopt me?"

She nodded solemnly. "I need someone to take over for me once I pass. I will not live forever. You have cooked for the clan while I rested. I know I can trust my recipes to you. And I would be proud to call you my son."

Tears filled my eyes and spilled over my cheeks. While my family was nowhere near as bad as Finn's, they were never very loving. I'd tried my whole life to make them proud and fell short no matter how hard I worked, how successful my business was. Nothing was good enough for them. And if they had ever found out I was in love with a man, they would not have hesitated to shun me to protect their image. Yamileth was offering me something I never thought to hope for. A family who wanted me, who was proud of me, who would accept every part of me. I never had to hide with her. She knew who I loved, and she accepted me anyway.

"I-I..." The words got caught in my throat, tears streaming down my cheeks and soaking her hands. She brushed them away with a smile, tipping her head at me.

"Is that a yes, sweet boy?"

I nodded rapidly, too choked up to form words. Yes. I wanted that. I wanted a real family.

She pinched my cheeks, smirking when I grimaced and leaned into her hands anyway. I'd take the rough treatment because she did it with love. And I didn't hate it.

"Well, then, good. I will introduce you to your brothers tomorrow. I have sent for them already. Tonight, you will spend time with your bondmate."

"B-brothers?" I spluttered. Instead of explaining, she just cackled, patting my cheek as she walked away. I gaped at her receding back, turning to face Verus when he snorted.

"She was waiting to do that," he chuckled, rolling his eyes affectionately.

Orthorr smirked and nodded in agreement. "I wouldn't doubt it. Now, Patrick, there is a ceremony to be adopted into a family, and another for bonding. Yamileth is already planning them both, so you need not worry about them. I agree that you should rest tonight. Yamileth's other sons are... rambunctious. You will need your energy to meet them."

I was too stunned to do anything but nod, letting Verus pull me to my feet and hand me my cane. He dipped his head at Orthorr, his expression unusually serious.

"Thank you, clan leader. It means a lot."

Orthorr gave him a soft smile in return. "I knew what he meant to you, Verus. I would have found some way to ensure your bonding. Now go. I've got no doubt that Yamileth will have all the elders in my tent soon to plan the ceremonies. I want to sneak some ale before they arrive."

Verus snickered, bowing with his fist against his chest before tugging me back outside. The cold rain was shocking, and my breath stuttered as we stepped out.

"Cold?" Verus asked, tugging me against his side.

"Yes. I didn't realize how warm I got when I was in there," I told him, snuggling against him.

He scooped me off my feet with a grin, smacking a kiss to my lips when I raised my eyebrows at him. "What? Did you think just because you can walk without crutches that I would let you walk around on your own? You are my ravsol. You deserve pampering."

Twenty-Six

After discussing the possibility of a curse with my brothers, I honestly hadn't thought things would work out so well once I got back. That Orthorr found a solution and got Patrick invited into the clan meant the world to me. I wanted to shout to the entire clan that this beautiful man was mine, but I realized while walking back to my tent that I hadn't asked him yet. Him being happy in the clan didn't mean he accepted me as his bondmate. I still had to ask.

Patrick was chilled from the rain when we ducked into my tent, so I stripped us both and dragged him under the furs to keep him warm. He immediately snuggled against me, and I marveled at how it felt for us to be wrapped around each other without him stuck on his back because of the splint.

"I missed you," he murmured, his voice muffled with his face pressed against my chest.

A smile stretched across my lips, and I hugged him tighter to me. "I missed you too, kolrav."

He made a questioning sound, wriggling to look up at me. "What does that word mean? And the other one, ravsol? I asked Finn, but he said he didn't know."

I hummed, thinking about it. It was hard to describe words I knew all my life. "Ravsol is used when the sun is setting. It is a term of endearment. I called you ravsol because of your hair."

Running my fingers through the copper strands, I smiled at his blush that highlighted the spots on his cheeks. Spots that covered his entire body. I found myself tracing them after each intimate moment. They were like stars scattered across his skin.

"And the other one?"

This one I knew because Rath told me the translation for it. He had to ask before he bonded with Finn, so he could better explain it to him.

"Kolrav is only used once, to the person we wish to bond with. In your language, it means 'my love'." Cupping his cheek, I rested my forehead against his. "In the clans, it is not the protector who chooses but the one he is protecting. It is your choice what we become. But should you wish it, I would ask that you bond with me. You are my other half, Patrick. I do not wish for us to part."

His eyes filled with tears and his chin trembled, but before I could worry about his reaction, he smiled so brightly, it warmed my soul.

"Yes! I choose you! I only want you! Really?"

Laughing, I nodded. "Yes, really. You are my Patrick. I would have followed you to your next destination if you'd asked it of me."

He shook his head, tears still streaming down his cheeks as he peppered me with kisses. "No. We'll stay here. I'm happy here. Unbelievably happy as long as I'm with you."

Capturing his lips, I kissed him roughly, too emotional to say more. I had everything I wanted, and I felt as though the joy was almost too much, that I would drown in it happily. It could not get better than this.

"Verus..." Patrick said between kisses, his fingers gripping my hair tightly.

"Mm?"

"Will you take me?" he whispered.

My eyes flew open, and I drew back enough to study him. His face was flushed bright red from the request. It was a first. Whenever we had been intimate before now, I always made the first move. I wanted him too much to hold back, and I was never known for being shy. Perhaps I should not have been so quick to make all the requests. It was hot hearing Patrick ask for me to take him.

Dipping my head, I tangled our tongues in a slow, sensual kiss. He moaned against my lips, pressing closer until there wasn't an inch of space between us. I could feel his hardness pressed against my hip. Knowing such a beautiful man desired me was a heady thought.

When I broke the kiss, Patrick chased me, a needy whimper in his throat. I chuckled, whispering against his lips.

"I want more than anything to take you, my Patrick. But…" I frowned, one hand sliding down to touch his injured leg. He still used a cane, and I'd seen him flinch when I helped him stand after talking to Orthorr. I did not wish to hurt him.

"I'm okay," he promised. "It's just a little uncomfortable."

It was uncomfortable now with him lying on his side and putting no pressure upon it. But if I took him as we were now, he'd end up on his back with his legs around my hips, and I knew it would hurt him to do so. Riding me would be even worse for him. I thought about it for a minute before pressing a kiss to Patrick's lips.

"Stay as you are. I have an idea."

He made a questioning sound, tracking me as I sat up and moved about. Keeping him on his side, I piled furs to support his leg before settling behind him. He glanced at me over his shoulder, a frown on his lips.

"Can it even be done this way?"

I could not help but smirk at him. "There are many ways that we can make love, my Patrick. I will show them all to you eventually."

His face flushed at my promise, but he came willingly when I settled his head against my shoulder and tipped his chin to capture his mouth again. I distracted him with kisses as I slicked my fingers with oil and ran them between his cheeks.

Knowing he was untouched made my blood boil with lust, but I took my time softening him, pushing my finger inside him a little at a time. He made delicious whimpering noises, pushing his hips back to seek more, but he did not rush me. He knew I only wished to take care of him. Sliding my finger in and out, I listened for any hints of pain or discomfort. I wanted it to be good for him.

Patrick's moans told me when it was okay for me to add another finger. He trembled in my arms, his hot breath panting against my lips. He didn't complain about the awkward angle. He stayed relaxed, trusting me with his body, and it made me fall harder for him. I could not help the words that spilled from me.

"You are so beautiful. So perfect. My kolrav, my gorgeous bondmate. I cannot wait to be inside you."

His moans grew louder, and he cried out when I twisted my fingers, running them along the front of his passage, where all men knew the key to pleasure resided. Patrick gripped my thigh roughly, his trembling growing more intense with each pass of my fingers.

"Verus! Verus, please!" he moaned, thrusting his hips to take my fingers. I grew desperate to be inside him, but I needed to stretch him first. I did not wish to hurt him.

Distracting him with kisses, I added a third finger, spreading them gently to make sure he was thoroughly stretched. I took care to avoid his pleasure spot as much as I could, since it felt as though he was close to completion already. If he came before I got inside him, I would feel proud of myself for getting him there, but I wished to be inside him first.

I was considering a fourth finger just to be thorough when Patrick jerked, gripping the base of his cock tightly. Knowing he was so close pushed me into action, and I pulled my fingers free, slicking my aching cock with the oil and dragging him back. Patrick's head lolled against my shoulder, his eyes glazed with lust and his breaths quick. It was a look I never wished to forget. Perhaps, if this round ended quickly, I could get him there again at least one more time tonight. Maybe twice. We had all night, after all.

I WAS TOO FAR GONE TO FOCUS ON WHAT VERUS WAS DOING. I'D GOTTEN SO close to release just from his fingers, and I was glad for the reprieve. My entire body thrummed with the need to come, and I could only hope I would last long enough for Verus to take me. I'd waited so long to experience it. I didn't want to miss it because I couldn't keep myself under control long enough for him to get inside me.

The hot, blunt tip of his cock slid along my crease, making me gasp and push my hips backward. The arm that was pillowing my head drew me closer to band across my chest, giving me something to cling to as Verus pushed inside me.

All the imaginings I had of being taken didn't come close to the reality. He went slow, easing in an inch at a time with small thrusts that had me squirming for more. I understood him wishing to keep me from experiencing any pain, but this was too slow, even for me.

"Verus... more..." I pleaded.

He groaned, resting his head against mine. "I do not wish to hurt you."

"It doesn't hurt," I promised him. "It feels good. So good. Please, Verus."

Letting out a harsh breath, his control slipped, and he thrust his hips forward, burying the remaining inches of his length inside me. We both stilled, groaning. I'd never felt so full in my life, and knowing it was Verus inside me nearly sent me over the edge.

Verus's head shook against my shoulder. "I'm sorry, kolrav. I can't—" He groaned deeply, pulling his hips back an inch and thrusting forward again. "I can't hold back. You are too perfect. I must—"

I encouraged him with a murmured, "Please...", clutching his arm as he drew back and thrust in again. Despite his words, he did not rush or get rough with me. His movements were steady, keeping him deep inside me and melting my insides. I almost wanted to beg for him to go faster, harder, my body craving more. But I also didn't wish for this to end. I wanted to be wrapped in him like this forever.

Verus's breath stuttered, and he reached around my hip, his free hand wrapping around my cock. The first stroke made my eyes roll back in my head. Feeling his cock inside me and his hand stroking me just right was too much for me to take for long. I gasped and moaned, thrusting my hips back to meet his, then forward to fuck into his fist. Tingles started at the base of my spine, spreading outward until I couldn't hold back anymore.

"Verus!"

"Oh, gods, yes!" Verus bellowed, his hips bucking against me as I came into his palm. The pleasure slammed into me hard like waves with every thrust of his hips until I went blind from the pleasure. I barely heard Verus shout with his release, but I swore I could feel it as he filled me. I shivered and moaned at the thought, letting the pleasure overwhelm me. I was safe in Verus's arms.

Twenty-Seven

Having slept alone while Verus was gone, I was overjoyed to wake up in his arms again. He'd kept me up late, eager and demanding for more. I gave him everything he asked for, until he took me into his mouth again, and the guilt over not reciprocating made me hesitate. It wasn't that I didn't trust him. I was just afraid of the pain. When I finally explained to him my hesitation, he was angry. Not with me, though. He wanted to go after Richard immediately and cut him down. It took wrapping myself around him to keep him from leaving in the middle of the night.

Once I had him settled, he explained to me that the way I experienced it was wrong, it wasn't supposed to be like that. And when I finally worked up the nerve to try it, he talked me through it and kept still, even though I could tell it was difficult for him. His thighs shook with the effort, and his fingers twisted in the furs so tightly his knuckles turned white. I would have felt guilty if he wasn't moaning and encouraging me, his head thrashing as he fought his instincts. When he came, I swallowed his release and was so turned on by the act I had to jerk myself off to get relief.

I loved that Verus gave me the opportunity to reclaim that moment for myself. Now that the act was no longer tainted with the memories of

Richard, I decided to wake Verus the same way, grinning to myself as he moaned and hardened in my mouth.

"Ravsol…" he breathed, his cock twitching between my lips.

I hummed, watching his face screw up with pleasure at the vibration. I was going to take him deeper when someone called out. Not to Verus. To me.

"Patrick?"

Releasing Verus's cock, I sat up, my head cocked. Why was Saneth visiting me so early?

Verus growled, sitting up abruptly. "What does he want?"

I realized belatedly that I'd never told Verus that Saneth had made amends, and we were friends now. Putting my hands up to stall him from starting a fight, I explained. "It's okay. He apologized while you were gone, and we've become friends. He isn't here to upset me."

Verus looked uncertain, but he trusted me not to lie to him. Pulling on trousers, I took Verus's hand when he helped me to my feet, calling out to Saneth as I rushed to get dressed.

"I'm coming!"

Verus scowled as he jerked his trousers up his legs, muttering under his breath. "No you aren't. We hadn't gotten to that part yet."

Snickering, I shoved his shoulder, tugging on my tunic. I looked disheveled and not very put together, but I figured Saneth would excuse me. He was the one waking me up.

When I stepped out of the tent, I stopped abruptly. Saneth was not alone. For a moment, I worried that Verus had been correct in assuming Saneth was here to cause trouble, since I hadn't interacted with Tavik since the last time he confronted me in the cooking tent. Saneth was quick to reassure me, his hands lifted in a soothing manner.

"He's here to apologize," he rushed out.

Verus stepped out behind me, his expression dark. He didn't trust Saneth's words. I didn't blame him. He hadn't been here for all the progress we'd made as friends. I laced my fingers with his, squeezing gently as a reminder that we were together, and I was safe with him. He squeezed back, his eyes never leaving the couple in front of us. Jerking his chin at Tavik, he glared at him.

"Go on, then."

Tavik scowled at him, but a sharp jab of Saneth's elbow in his belly kept him from saying anything rude. He grunted, rubbing the spot, and frowned at Saneth.

"Ouch."

Saneth rolled his eyes. "Don't pretend it hurt. You promised, Tavik."

With a long suffering sigh, Tavik nodded and turned to face me. "I wanted to apologize. I let my jealousies blind me from the truth and was unjustly cruel to you. Saneth told me what you did for us. Had you not befriended him, I might not have ever found my happiness. So I'm sorry. And thank you for hearing his words."

I dipped my chin to acknowledge him. "Thank you for apologizing. Saneth is my friend. I'm glad he found the courage to tell you how he felt."

Tavik turned a soft look on his friend, who rolled his eyes and elbowed him again. "Okay, we will leave you be now. I thought I would find you in the cooking tent since breakfast is soon. I'm sorry if I woke you."

Surprised, I whipped my gaze skyward. The sky was bright, and the sun was over the horizon. I was late.

Sucking in a sharp breath, I whirled around, rushing back into the tent to grab my cane. Verus snatched me around the waist as I tried to hurry past him, tucking me against his side.

"Ravsol? Where are you going?"

"I'm late!" I screeched, wriggling free of his hold. "You kept me up too late!"

I heard his laugh behind me as I practically ran for the cooking tent. I would have run outright if the pain in my leg would allow it. Instead, I walked quickly with the help of the cane, and hoped Yamileth wouldn't regret agreeing to adopt someone so careless.

THANKFULLY, YAMILETH WASN'T ANGRY WITH ME. SHE DID TEASE ME mercilessly, pointing out a bruise on my neck that Verus had put there with his mouth the night prior. I took the teasing in stride, just grateful she wasn't angry with me.

We got breakfast out on time and made preparations for lunch and supper before she dragged me from the cooking tent to meet her sons. I was nervous to meet them, worried they'd protest someone so soft joining their family, but they were a friendly bunch. The older two were warriors who had moved to another village to experience the world. The youngest was a scout and not with the clan very often. It was a matter of luck that he happened to be home in time for the adoption ceremony. I was apparently going to be the only son of Yamileth's that didn't feel the urge to wander.

"So, Patrick. Our mother rarely compliments someone else's cooking. It's high praise that she's willing to eat your food. Will you make us a meal?" Rheinris, the middle child, asked with a grin.

Yamileth whacked him across the back of the head, scowling at him. "He is not your personal cook. Behave."

Rheinris rubbed the sore spot with a frown at his mother. "We're to be his family. Isn't it only fair we get to try this food you keep praising so much?"

I felt my cheeks flush as they continued to bicker. I had no idea Yamileth talked about me to them. I thought she would just tell them her intentions. That she would praise my cooking meant the world to me.

Daezal, the youngest, leaned to whisper to me. "If you wish to stay out of trouble, beware of Rheinris. He enjoys pushing our mother's buttons."

"Is there a reason?" I asked quietly.

He rolled his eyes, taking a sip of his ale. "He says it is because Father asked him to keep her on her toes. I think he just enjoys the attention."

"Like you're any better," Jakr growled.

He'd been a little intimidating when I first met him, easily the same size as Tavik, but his handshake had been gentle and he yanked Rheinris away when he tried to wrestle with me upon our first meeting. He was protective by nature, and that seemed to extend to me now.

Daezal pouted at his eldest brother. "I am. I do not purposely irritate her."

"No, you just do it without thinking about it. You are the reason she has gray hairs."

Pursing my lips, I fought back a snicker. Orthorr had been right that they were a rambunctious group, but despite the frown on Yamileth's face, she was pleased to have her sons with her.

Verus poked his head into Yamileth's tent, his eyebrows raised. "Are you ready?"

Sucking in an unsteady breath, I nodded. Yamileth refused to leave the ceremony to adopt me into her family until a later time. She wanted me brought into the clan as soon as possible. Which was why she gave control of the cooking to someone else. She was the head of her family, so she needed to be there. She was none too pleased about not being the one to cook dinner, and I got the feeling after the ceremony was over, she'd be back in that tent to watch over things.

Yamileth and her sons left the tent first, each of them patting Verus's shoulder as they walked past. They knew who he was to me; I didn't hide it when I met them. I told them of my intention to bond with him. They were looking forward to that ceremony. Apparently, there was a lot more alcohol involved in that one.

Verus offered me his arm when I finally came to stand beside him. I took it, leaning into him when he kissed my temple.

"Relax, ravsol. The clan already loves you. I've heard nothing but praise about your cooking and your kindness while I was away. This is just to make things official."

"You promise?" I couldn't help but ask, my voice unsteady. Even when my business was doing well in my old town, I wasn't well liked. People put up with me because my food was good. They never would have had a celebration for me, no matter the occasion. And no one would invite me into their families willingly. My own wanted little to do with me. And I wasn't unaware that none had come looking for me since I ran away. Finn told me his brother came to fetch him; I knew it was possible for them to figure it out. They didn't care enough to do that.

I wouldn't have gone with them even if they had. This was my home now. After this ceremony, I would have a family who cared for me, a clan who would protect me, and the man I loved at my side. If there was a better recipe for a happy life, I couldn't think of one.

"I promise, my Patrick. Are you ready?"

"I'm ready," I agreed, squeezing his arm as he led me toward the village center where the ceremony would take place.

It turned out running away from my home was the best decision I ever made.

Did you find a typo?

This book has been edited and reviewed to find any typos and mistakes, but alas, we are only human. If you spot an error, please let me know! I want to hear from you so I can fix it!

Send me an email at authoramypadilla@gmail.com or send me a message on my Facebook group page.

Also by Amy Padilla

DALLYING WITH DEMONS

Dating a Demon

Taming a Demon

Claiming a Demon

Loving a Demon

Saving a Demon

∼

CHARMED AWAY TEMP AGENCY

The Incubus's Assistant

The Dragon's Aide

The Shapeshifter's Secretary

The Vampire's Receptionist

The Telepath's Associate

∼

NOT-SO-SAVAGE BARBARIANS

The Barbarian's Tribute

Saved by a Barbarian

Seducing a Barbarian

The Barbarian's Claim

The Physician's Barbarian

The Barbarian Prince

About the Author

Amy is an introverted squish who loves Happily Ever Afters, Magic, and True Love. While she doesn't stick with one specific subgenre, her favorite tends to be fluffy paranormal romance. In between writing books (like several. At one time. Because squirrel.) Amy likes to read and play relaxing video games. Her kindle is stuffed with romance and she hoards trophy books on her shelves. You can find her most nights pretending to be fancy with a glass of sparkling cider and a good book.

Send her a message. She might be an introvert, but she won't resist being adopted by an extrovert.

Don't forget to join her Facebook group for the latest updates and more!

Sign up for her newsletter on her website to get more news and occasional shorts.

www.ingramcontent.com/pod-product-compliance
Lightning Source LLC
Chambersburg PA
CBHW020507060426
42491CB00001B/50